Cannes, 1900, All Saints Day!
The girl brought her hand out of the pocket of
her coat and showed him that it held a little
pistol. She didn't quite point it, she waited for
his fear or anger to suck it towards him. It was
nickel-plated and reflected the light from the
table lamp beside his chair. The lamps were lit; it
was such a dark day.
The Judge found to his surprise that he didn't feel
any emotion. He wondered, could it be that he
was brave and had never known it? 'Please go
away,' he said, and rang the service bell placed in
the wall . . . The waiter took in the situation and
shouted, 'Hey you!' The girl stood still, and he
leaped at her and hit her with his tray. The girl
kicked him. The little pistol went off, and the
bullet entered the Judge's body just below his
midriff . . .

The Petersburg-Cannes Express

Express

HANS KONING

SPHERE BOOKS LIMITED
30/32 Gray's Inn Road, London WC1X 8JL

First published in Great Britain by Hamish Hamilton Ltd, 1975
Copyright © 1975 by Hans Koning
First published by Sphere Books Ltd, 1980

The quote by Joachim du Bellay is from his:

Heureux qui, comme Ulysse, a fait un beau voyage,
Ou come cestuy la qui conquit la toison,
Et puis est retourné, plein d'usage et raison,
Vivre entre ses parent le reste de son aagel

in a translation by the author.

The song 'Je Cherche Fortune' (Le Chat Noir) was published by
Editions Salabert, Paris.

TRADE
MARK

Set in Monotype Garamond

Printed in Great Britain by
William Collins Sons & Co Ltd
Glasgow

Lucky who, like Ulysses, has made a seemly journey,
Hence wisely has gone home —

JOACHIM DU BELLAY

I. Cannes, a judge

Before the Judge was even fully awake, he knew that it had been raining all night and that the rain was coming down as hard as ever. He had slept badly, the gurgling and dripping of the water outside the balcony doors of his French hotel room had bothered him. He opened his eyes and lay still, looking up in the half-light at the stucco cherubim which smiled at him from the ceiling. He thought – it was not simple to say what. The Judge usually thought in images rather than in formulated ideas; it would have surprised his enemies that this man, who had sent so many to hard labour, had so few precise thoughts.

The Judge rang for his breakfast. He conjured up a picture of his supper of the night before and then, uneasily, of his own innards such as he had seen them depicted in the medical encyclopedia in his doctor's waiting room. Why had they used such lurid colours, why these purple and blue intestines? He thought of the baboons in the Saint Petersburg zoo, and then of his mother's legs not long before she died, with their blue and black spots, varicose veins.

He put his hand on his belly. The Judge, president of the Petersburg District Court, had come for a stay in Cannes on the advice of his doctor, who had spoken highly of the cooking (delicious but not heavy like Russian food) and of the good effect on the nerves of sodium chloride in the air. The Judge had liked the sound of that word, sodium chloride. There was something sunny about it. The doctor had also said, mistakenly as it turned out, that it seldom rained in the south of France.

The Judge was fond of his doctor, precisely because that

man always talked about climate, nerves, sea air, bland or stimulating foods, and never of diseases, lesions, operations.

'Why is it raining again?' the Judge asked the waiter, who put the breakfast tray on his bed and then went to draw the curtains. 'It's freakish, sir, I assure you,' the waiter answered. 'I've worked here for twenty years, I've never seen it like this.' He peered over the grey, smooth sea and announced, 'It will clear before noon, it's already getting lighter over La Napoule.'

'Well, it better,' said the Judge. He had looked forward to wearing his new taupe suit and suede shoes.

It didn't clear, and the Judge did not have a pleasant luncheon. He stayed in the hotel. Outside the windows of the dining-room, the sea boulevard, the Croisette, lay empty under the rain. Though he didn't know, it was Toussaint, All Saints' Day, one of France's most solemn holidays. It was the first of November of the year 1900. Our century had begun.

The Judge decided to cheer himself up with crêpes Suzette and a glass of marc. But just as he had given the order, his pain reappeared: the spasms and twinges that had sent him to his Petersburg doctor and from there on to France.

He put his napkin on the table and pushed his chair back. He was scared. But I've lived my life, he told himself. Ten years, I settle for just ten more years. My new house. Comfortable years. He tried visualising his own tombstone, tried seeing the dates on it. Could he make it 1835–1910? Yes, it said 1910. He had ten more years. Then the pain had vanished, and he dismissed the whole business.

But I won't have those crêpes, he thought. I'll very quietly go and smoke a cigar. Nurse the nervous system. Those had been his doctor's words.

He stood up and leaned his hand for a moment against the moist windowpane. The sea was so still that he could see the circles drawn on it by the heavy drops. The flagstones of the deserted hotel terrace gleamed, a miserable horse and cart creaked by, the contours of the hills across the bay stood sharply drawn, dark green, against the sky. With the winter

8

season people arriving, it would all be more cheerful. He turned and walked through the empty dining-room to the smoking lounge, off the lobby.

As he took his first puff, leaning back with closed eyes in his easy chair, he smelled the dining-room waiter again. One of the annoyances of his lunch had been the smell of wet clothes that had hung around that waiter. Was the fellow following him around now with those damned crêpes? Reluctantly he opened his eyes.

But it wasn't the waiter he had smelled, it was a girl or young woman, in a long, dripping raincoat, who stood in front of him.

'Judge,' the girl said in Russian.

The Judge looked from her face to the carpet, where a puddle was forming. The sight made him frown.

'I – ' the girl said, 'am Sophia Derkheim.' And when he did not react, 'The sister of Michael Derkheim.'

The Judge frowned again. He did not recognise the name but it held an unpleasant association. Or it was the girl, the wet carpet.

'You sentenced my brother to six years at hard labour,' the girl told him, 'and he was innocent. Last month we got word that he had died.'

A long face, brown hair. The Judge saw this boy now (though he wasn't completely sure), yes, he had looked like his sister. He felt a flush of pity, not connected with the dead, vague, brother, but because the girl was so ungainly. The human condition. Perhaps she deserved to be loved, or at least to be desired, but those feet, that bony forehead –

He was innocent, she said. The persons in front of him played their roles, he played his role, like threshing, where the peasants did throw their grain or whatever it was in the air, and let the wind – He sighed, he didn't say anything.

The girl brought her hand out of the pocket of her coat and showed him that it held a little pistol. She didn't quite point it, she waited for his fear or anger to suck it towards him. It was nickel-plated and reflected the light from the

9

table lamp beside his chair. The lamps were lit; it was such a dark day.

The Judge found to his surprise that he didn't feel any emotion. He wondered, could it be that he was brave and had never known it? 'Please go away,' he said, and rang the service bell placed in the wall.

'I thought you . . . This is even worse,' the girl said half aloud.

He made a gesture, and unexpectedly a shiver went through him which made him drop his cigar.

The girl looked at it and at him. 'Oh for God's sake,' she muttered and turned away.

I wonder if I should go and report her, the Judge already thought. He saw himself waiting endlessly on wooden benches in French police stations.

But then the summoned waiter appeared from behind the Japanese screen that hid the service door. Chance had that it wasn't Albert, the old smoking-room waiter. who was visiting his wife's grave for All Saints Day. but an apprentice recently hired on probation, a young man with athletic aspirations.

This man took in the situation and shouted, 'Hey you!' The girl stood still, and he leaped at her and hit her with his tray. The girl kicked him. The little pistol went off. and the bullet entered the Judge's body just below his midriff.

II. Marseilles, Sophia

A month later, on Monday, 3 December 1900, Sophia Derkheim was brought to trial before an Assizes Court convened without jury in Marseilles.

This unusual haste was due to the pushing of the local

prefect, who wanted the affair out of the way before the Riviera started its winter season.

The president of the court, though, wasn't pleased at all with such considerations. especially as it was still unclear whether the victim of Sophia's bullet, now in the Hildes-heimer private clinic in Super-Cannes, would survive – a mood of the court which would work in her favour.

The French newspapers, after an initial flurry, didn't show much interest in the case. Sophia Derkheim was too awkward for them, too badly dressed, and too silent. What could you make of a girl who seemed to wear size-ten shoes, and whose victim, a draining tube sticking out from under his sheet, only talked about his liquid diet? The Figaro had begun its coverage by juxtaposing French justice and Russian tyranny and painting Sophia in rather heroic colours, but the Sociétés des Bains de Mer and the hotel syndicates put an end to that: the owner of the paper held shares in some of these enter-prises and they would assuredly not profit from giving rich Russian tourists the idea that terrorism was being cham-pioned in France.

In Petersburg it was different, the case was a sensation. The editorials showed the appropriate indignation, mixed with a touch of gratitude towards Providence for staging this outrage on the soil of France, 'a nation not innocent in its past of sowing the seeds of anarchy'. A salutary lesson.

But then the Marseilles court allowed Sophia's lawyer to cross-examine her on motive and to drag in her brother's story. The day after that, there was even laughter in the courtroom, unchecked by the president, as the athletic waiter was on the stand with his silver tray. The papers, sensitive like seismographs, changed their tone. Could it be that even high judicial officers of Russia's ally France were tainted with anarchism?

Suddenly it was all over, with Sophia Derkheim sent to jail for one ridiculous year. After a day of silence, every Russian paper printed its editorial outcry.

The French Ambassador in Petersburg was summoned to the long, low building across from the Winter Palace, where the Russian Minister for Foreign Affairs sits, and an obscure communiqué issued afterwards spoke of 'a meeting of the minds in the matter of the criminal convict S. Derkheim'.

That communiqué worried Sophia's friends in Petersburg. They had been in the middle of a little celebration over the outcome of the trial, when one of them came in with the afternoon paper and read it out to them.

What could this meeting of the minds mean, except some kind of foul play?

The French legal system was truly independent of government interference, a girl said.

All governments and all government institutions were the same, she was told, when you scraped off the varnish, they were all full of scoundrels.

The verdict celebration party had lost its steam at this point. Soon everyone went home.

III. Saint Petersburg, Anna

Among them was a twenty-five-year-old teacher named Anna, an ex-classmate of Sophia's in high school.

Those two had not kept in close touch, and that Cannes drama had seemed rather pointless to Anna; but she had belonged to a small group of friends of Sophia's brother Michael. Anna had liked him very much, and right then she was the only one who decided to try and do something for Sophia.

Anna knew Sophia's and Michael's mother and the state that woman had been in during the past weeks. It was Anna who had taken her a bunch of flowers with the happy news about Sophia's one-year sentence.

And this same evening she was supposed to go back and

have dinner there. A terrible idea, to sit across from Sophia's mother and either pretend all was well, or pick at that phrase about the meeting of the minds with her and speculate what it could mean.

It was a miserable afternoon, twilight already brought on by great wet snowflakes which crept into the collar of her ratty fur coat, carts and horse-drawn cabs splashing everyone with brown mud.

As she took her place in line at the streetcar stop, a thin and shabby man came up to her and said, 'Ann. It's me.' She didn't recognise him until he took off his large hat which looked as if he had cut it out himself.

'Oh, Tolcheff, Andrew Tolcheff. Where did you come from?'

'I was lying in wait, I want to talk to you. I live very close by now. Do you mind?'

This was a strange man by all accounts, a free-lance journalist of no clear income, class, or even nationality. He was supposed to be the son of a long since vanished American, a seaman maybe, and a Russian or possibly Gypsy mother; he knew everybody and was known as a 'fixer', but never seemed after money in his enterprises. His sister, a great beauty, had surprisingly married a Second Secretary of the American Embassy and wanted to forget all about him and their origins, but the Second Secretary himself liked to lend Tolcheff a spare suit of evening clothes and take him to diplomatic functions.

Tolcheff brought Anna to a cold and smoky apartment, where a girl in a long black dress was reading a book, huddled near a fireplace burning crates and magazines. 'Wenda – Ann,' Tolcheff murmured.

'You read about the meeting-of-minds?' he asked Anna.

She nodded and asked, 'Why didn't you come up to our party?'

'They're not too fond of me. I hardly knew the girl.'

'But you knew Michael well, didn't you?'

'Yes. Yes, very well,' Tolcheff said, with what Anna thought was a somewhat stagy melancholy. 'In fact, I should have been – he took on – ' His voice trailed off.

'Don't talk nonsense, André,' the other girl said, but he paid no attention to her.

'I must help Sophia if it's the last thing I do,' he said. 'Do you understand what it is all about?'

'No,' Anna answered. 'But you do.'

'The word is,' Tolcheff announced, 'that Petersburg fears an epidemic of attacks, outrages as they call it, if Sophia gets away with one year. Specially abroad. Our officials will be afraid to go on their well-earned Mediterranean vacations. They feel that the French court came near to saying Sophia had been right.'

'They can't make it change its verdict.'

'No, no,' Tolcheff agreed hastily, 'but the French government isn't too happy with it either. What they talked about at the Ministry is, they're going to send a big shot to Marseilles, to demand of the court that it suspend its sentence and extradite convict Derkheim to Russia. Nothing governmental, you see, purely legal, and with precedents. And they'll try her again here and let her rot and die in the same cell in Simbirskaya prison that her brother had.'

'Oh. Goddammit. You know, when you came up to me at the stop, I was on my way to see the dean of our old school. She was fond of Sophia.'

Tolcheff made a face.

'The dean has a lot of pull,' Anna said. 'She has connections who – '

'The case is handled by a man called Draskovich,' he interrupted. 'Undersecretary of the Interior, and head of what used to be called until four years ago, the Third Section, the secret state police. He's the man to see, and I am going to see him.'

'Are you serious?'

'In his office he's just a civil servant,' Tolcheff told her. 'I've studied him at a reception, in his London-tailor suit, telling dirty stories. He likes to be taken for a foreign diplomat. He's a little snob. Nothing to be afraid of. You see, he is lazy, he hates fuss and bother.'

'Is that good?'

'You bet. And that is where I need your help. Because you're on the youth council and all that stuff, aren't you?'

'How do you know so much?' she asked.

He ignored that. 'He's supposed to have said once, "Ten freshman students on a street corner can ruin my career." I want to tell him to leave well enough alone. Not tell him, make him think it himself. If he brings Derkheim back, there'll be demonstrations, school strikes, all sorts of trouble, just the opposite of what they want to achieve.'

'There will be?'

'According to the secret report from the youth council. Written by you and me. Will you help? There's no risk for you, or very little.'

That annoyed Anna. 'Does Draskovich know who you are?' she asked.

'He once told my sister that he couldn't understand how such an unpleasant type, I, could have such a beautiful sister, she. But that was his idea of a compliment. He thinks of himself as a devil with women.'

'How would you get to see him?'

'I have an in at the Ministry. Well, do you approve?'

She thought about it. 'Up to a point. I'm willing to write the report with you, I mean fake a report. But let me take it to him. I think we'd stand a better chance.'

Tolcheff looked somewhat superiorly amused. 'Because of the ladies' man angle?'

'No – because you say he's a snob. He must know my father was in the Foreign Service; he'll at least be polite.'

Tolcheff reddened for a moment. 'Very well, you go.'

IV. Saint Petersburg, the Undersecretary

That was bitchy of me, she had thought afterwards, but then
he shouldn't always act so damn clever. Anyway, a girl will
do better with Draskovich than a journalist without newspaper.

Draskovich didn't keep her waiting. His large, panelled
office sat oddly at the end of a grubby corridor.

He doesn't look phoney or sinister; he's a bit like Tolcheff,
a well-fed, groomed Andrew Tolcheff. She found it easy to
say what she had meant to say.

He listened without interrupting, attentively, and he
accepted the report they had concocted.

He didn't look at it.

'You young people surely have your ear to the ground,'
he then said. 'Or maybe the proper phrase is, your fingers in
all the pies. Tell me, young lady, do you personally know
this Sophia Derkheim?'

'We were in school together.'

'So you're here as her advocate so to speak. You can be
open with me.'

'I – ' Anna began.

'Or is it the public interest the youth council is after?'
Draskovich asked.

'The two happen to coincide,' Anna said, pleased with
that answer. 'Not that her family hasn't suffered enough.'

'Hmm, I see,' he said and seemed lost in thought.

I think we're pulling it off, Anna told herself.

Draskovich started biting his thumbnail and she tried not
to stare at that. 'Perhaps your friend Andy the Fix isn't as
clever as he thinks he is,' he suddenly said, in a different, loud
voice.

'I don't know what you mean, Mr Undersecretary.'

He swivelled his chair around, away from her, and looked out of the window behind him. 'No, I'm sure you don't,' he said. 'I'll share a little secret with you. When I come back, I'll have you both up for conspiracy.' He turned again and smiled at her. 'So don't go anywhere.'

Anna swallowed and opened her mouth to protest.

Draskovich quickly continued, 'Come back from where, you'll wonder. Back from France. I'm going there myself, this coming Sunday, to make sure nothing goes wrong with the extradition. Also because I need a change of scenery. The winter here is very tiresome, don't you agree?'

Anna stared at him.

'Don't you agree?' he insisted.

'I like winter.'

Draskovich gave a little laugh. 'She likes winter,' he said to the window, turning his back on her again. 'God, they're sure diplomats, they sure know how to handle people. Honest to the bitter end, eh, just to put me to shame. Is that the recipe Andy the Fix had for me? You people give me a pain in the neck. And as for the family Derkheim having suffered enough – shall I tell you something?'

The expression on his face frightened her. His dirty stories. A picture in an old book, a barber opening an artery, people watching curiously –

'I'll let you into another little secret,' he said. 'I don't think they have suffered enough. I think people like those Derkheims are bad blood, rotten apples. I think it's in the best interest of the country that the Derkheim line dies out right now, that it finds its end in Miss Sophia Derkheim's maidenish womb. I assume it's maidenish?'

'We'll see it stays just that,' he went on when Anna did not answer. 'It'll go maidenish into the grave.'

Anna got up.

'Yes, you people give me a pain.' Draskovich's voice went into a higher pitch. 'You came here full of nobility, didn't you, a little mission to save your friend, just a few smiles and Draskovich will jump through the hoop. Do you think that's how life is? Is that the best you can do for your friends? We do better for ours, I assure you.'

'I will do anything you can think of, to help Sophia,' Anna said slowly.

'You will? Now you interest me. Are you good?'

Anna felt that she blushed and cursed herself soundlessly.

'Let's see your breasts,' he said.

She immediately dropped her jacket on the chair, opened her blouse, undid her bra and pulled it out from underneath.

'Too small,' Draskovich said. 'Bad luck for Sophia,' and he rang the bell on his desk.

Anna slipped into her coat, and with her jacket and bra in one hand, walked out past a secretary who came in from the corridor.

V. Saint Petersburg, the railroad station

It was nine in the evening but here at the edge of the city it was night, a countryside winter night with the east wind blowing in unchecked from the fields, rattling the fences of the empty cattle yards and too cold even to carry the stench from the slaughterhouse behind them. Only in front of the railroad station, over the circle where the streetcars coming down from Izmailovski Prospect made their turns, was a pool of light, extended in each direction by a lost row of street lamps along a canal.

The travellers for the last local trains of the day, to Pskov and Gatchina, struggled with their bundles against the wind to get to the station entrance and into the dismal waiting room, where on a Sunday night only two stoves were kept going, with a policeman to make sure no heat reached any unqualified persons.

Beyond the ticket gates lay the platforms under the glass dome, empty, in a bluish light interrupted by the smoke from shunting engines.

On the edge of this iron, coal dust, and cold was the other world, the first-class waiting room and restaurant, with a yellow glow shining through its frosted windows, waves of warmth coming out when a porter opened the door.

In the red stone façade, the names were chiselled of towns served from here, Pskov, Dvinsk, Riga, Vilna, and Warsaw, which gave it its name, Warsaw Station. It was the terminal from which the new winter express, established two years before in 1898, left every Sunday and Thursday, via Warsaw, Vienna, Venice, and Milan, to Monte Carlo, Nice, and Cannes, first class only, in a sixty-four-hour journey, true miracle of the twentieth century ahead, the dignitaries had said in their speeches. A beautiful, sleek train, with its blue dining cars and oak-panelled sleepers with the golden lettering: Compagnie Internationale des Wagons-lits et des Grands Express Européens.

This was the train the Undersecretary was taking to get Sophia Derkheim extradited and into a Russian grave, as he had said.

He was travelling alone, though he had been offered a clerk to accompany him. He didn't want anyone breathing down his neck during the vacation in Cannes he had mapped out for himself, in combination with his mission.

Draskovich had arrived early for he disliked hurry and bustle. He was having a drink in the restaurant while a porter was putting his luggage in his compartment, nice leather pieces, neither too old nor too new. He felt a genuine warmth then towards himself and towards his fellow men and women, the few small groups sitting around with friends seeing them off. He had entered the restaurant from the frozen city as a civil servant, a police bureaucrat, with a detective at his heels by way of bodyguard just in case; he'd walk out through the other door on to the platform where the express was waiting, an international traveller with luggage from Bond Street, a man who could be anybody, go anywhere on earth, without enemies, to sunny places, to the most expensive hotels, and the vilest bars.

He smiled in the mirrored wall beside him. There was something unbelievably lucky about his life. I must admit, he thought, that keeping down a bunch of students and other slobs with crazy ideas about the world is rewarded extravagantly by my fellow citizens. But there you are, they're afraid, they pay so as not to be afraid. They set the price, not I.

It said ten on the big clock behind the buffet. A small one next to it showed one minute to eight and a brass plaque underneath read, 'Greenwich Mean Time'. He repeated those words with pleasure. He'd wait to board the train until the first bell at ten fifteen, stroll past the coaches, alone, without showing awareness of the passengers behind the windows staring, the family farewell wavings. His coat over his right arm, the astrakhan fur collar out. People would wonder who he was.

Draskovich's moves were being followed. He didn't know, and if he had, he wouldn't have cared, for he felt great contempt for all his enemies. And it doubtlessly looked a clumsy plan that at the same hour had brought Andrew Tolcheff in a nondescript kind of railroad uniform to a service shack on the platform, while Anna, late and shivering with nervousness, was on her way to the station in a Number 9 streetcar.

She was wearing a hat and a long black dress provided by Tolcheff (she thought she recognized it as the dress of the girl at his smoky fire place). He had assumed Anna would have a nice wardrobe and was surprised when she told him she didn't, and hadn't been home to her father in six years. The hat, which she disliked particularly, was of black velvet with an upturned brim; she still wore her own scraggly rabbit fur coat.

Two days earlier, after her Draskovich interview, Anna had found herself hurrying back to Tolcheff's apartment, so miserable and angry at herself that she had to talk about it.

She didn't tell him the final episode. Tolcheff's immediate reaction had been, 'Let's follow him, let's get on his train with him.' Why? To do something, to get the better of him somehow. It was a long journey, a chance would come up. Anna had only shrugged, wiped her eyes, and left.

But then Tolcheff, surpassing himself, had found out Draskovich's schedule (bad news that he was taking this new, fast train), had managed to steal his sister's old Russian passport for Anna, had procured two hundred roubles for her ticket, had convinced her that she should ask her school for early Christmas vacation on medical grounds, and had generally bamboozled her into agreeing to his plan – although she had no idea what exactly it consisted of. He was obscure about his own moves, he'd be on the train, not as a passenger which was too risky, but in the service van: he had friends among the personnel.

It sounded idiotic to her. But he said he needed her help, and that was soothing. She had to do something, anything, to fight her disgust. Draskovich as he talked of Sophia's womb – a confused nightmare Anna often had, about death and children; walking out of that office into a wooden corridor with its poison-green walls, holding her bra in her hand –

Tolcheff had assured her there wasn't a chance that Draskovich would spot her. The train, so early in the season, was more than half empty. Draskovich had reserved a whole compartment for himself, one of the best, up front right behind the first dining car. 'You do know everything,' she had said with a certain bitterness, and Tolcheff had nodded. She shouldn't eat in either of the dining cars; he'd bring her tea and sandwiches from the pantry in the service van. Had he been on those trains before? No, but he didn't have to, he had seen the diagrams. Anna could act a sickly lady, lying low.

'And what do we do when we're there?' she had asked. 'As far as I'm concerned, I've twenty roubles left, which is, what, fifty francs.'

'Don't worry about it,' he had answered, 'we're only going part of the way, as far as the frontier. I have friends there.'

She was a bit fed up with those friends of his everywhere.

It was twenty minutes past ten when Anna hurried into the station with her little suitcase, waving away a porter, passed the inspection, and came on to the platform – an odd appearance, stared at by the employees. She got into the first compartment of the rear car, where she had the upper berth. The lower one was not taken, but when she decided she preferred it and put her things on it, the attendant came in from the corridor and told her that was against the rules. He was clearly just waiting for a tip to waive those rules, but she was in such a foul mood at this point, her feet frozen in the idiotic black pumps she was wearing to be in style with her role, bewildered by her own decision to be there, on this inimical train, that she snapped, 'Right', grabbed her possessions off the lower berth, and tossed them on to the upper one, where her toilet case hit the wall with a sound of breaking glass. I bet you Tolcheff isn't even on this damn train, she thought with such fury as if she were already sure of that.

She lowered the blind, took off her dress and shoes and stockings, and crept under the blankets, tucking them in around her feet. When she turned off the lamp from her bed, a blue night light flicked on, slowly drawing out of the darkness the shapes of her compartment, the curtains, the hissing steam radiator, the cupboard containing the wash-basin, two glasses in holders, and enamelled instructions in French, Russian, English, and German.

The last bell, a whistle, and the train pulled out very smoothly. It was half past ten Saint Petersburg time.

After a while, she scrambled over on her berth and raised the blind. The woods and the low hills that ringed the bay of Petersburg stood out black against a whitish sky, as cold as the moon itself, which shone above them in a hazy ring.

Not a light showed; an endless, deserted world.

VI. Between Saint Petersburg and Vilna

When Anna woke up, it was still dark. The train had stopped. She peered around the blind and wiped the vapour off the window: an empty station platform, echoing steps of a mechanic with a large hammer, a glass-walled control cabin with a bench on which a man sat beside a little stove, chewing bread, staring ahead.

The name sign said, Dunaburg-Dvinsk. It was almost half past seven on the station clock.

The banging of a carriage door.

She saw a clear sequence of images, of how it was to live in this town, to get up at six in the black winter morning, to walk through the snowy, deserted streets to the railroad station, to start a day there as a signalman, pulling out your breakfast wrapped in a piece of newspaper, the images were as sharp as photographs, and yet she felt this town was so far from anything she knew, so lost in vastness, that it made her dizzy; she could not take her eyes off that man. Then she heard a whistle, the train started to move, and he did not stir, he never looked up.

She crawled back under her blankets, after having reached over for her fur coat and put it on her feet. The train crossed an iron bridge. The Dvina, she said to herself, I'm not a schoolteacher for nothing, something about Lithuanian knights. She was happy with the rhythm of the bridge girders, a reassuring enclosure, then suddenly the sound ended. She had to look, it was a pine wood coming to within a few feet of the track, like a silent tunnel.

She fell into a reverie. She had never been out of Petersburg, or not since she was a child, but she didn't feel as if the train were carrying her away from anything, she felt safer with each mile left behind. Not, surely, she thought, because of Draskovich and his threat about conspiracy. It was a funny idea, here she was only a hundred feet or so away from him. But she didn't think long about him or Sophia or any of that. For the first time in perhaps a year she thought about her own childhood, her father, to whom she so easily had said good-bye when he didn't approve of her, and she not of him. No, not easily; but she had been determined never to let the fear of being alone direct her. Then it seemed she'd used up her courage in that and had started fooling herself. As if you were less alone, as if you were not alone, when you had someone to touch you. The universe. A crystal void, those were the words she used in her thoughts, eternal sunshine, not even eternal, burning out. Here I am, my poor body lost in that endlessness. And as an antidote against being scared, another body against mine. Worse than stupid, weak.

Since, she had been so busy, convinced of the rightness and usefulness of her work. She still was. Only for children can we mitigate the shock –

But now, in the security of the metal shell of this train, she was overcome by a kind of melancholy. A tenderness for herself as a child, when life was softer and warmer. She slept.

When she opened her eyes again, a hesitant daylight came around the edges of the blind, and when she raised it, she saw that they were rolling through a foggy landscape of wet snow falling on bare fields.

She put her coat and shoes on, and after making sure the corridor was empty, she scurried to the toilet, and then back to her compartment and back in bed. There was a knock on the door, and when she had unbolted it from the bed, an attendant came in and put a tray with a glass of tea on the little side table. She peered at him over her blanket and said she was not well and not to be disturbed any more.

Then there was another knock, and in came Tolcheff, who looked pleased with himself. He locked the door behind him and climbed up to sit on the foot of her berth.

'So you are on the train, Tolcheff.' Anna said.

'It's a beauty. God, how these people live! All this velvet and furs and mahogany flying past those filthy villages . . . ! Are you ready to hear our plan? Wait, let me give you your breakfast first.'

He pulled two rolls and a chocolate bar out of the pocket of his grey uniform jacket, and placed them on the bed.

'Are you sure I can be told why I'm here?' she asked, but she smiled. She couldn't help being pleased with her adventure suddenly. And Tolcheff looked different from Petersburg, nicer, though she couldn't tell why. Perhaps he should have been a railroad man.

'You might have been stopped at the station control,' he said. 'It was safer for you not to know anything.'

She nodded and unwrapped her chocolate.

'We,' Tolcheff announced solemnly, 'you and I, and two other men, are going to kidnap Draskovich.'

'Oh no. Not me,' she said promptly.

'Two friends of mine will be waiting for us at Granitsa. They're on their way there now, from Warsaw. Granitsa, as you may know, is the Russian border station for this railroad line, and for most of the southern section.'

'Please go on.'

Tolcheff, though, liked to unfold his plans; he saw it that way, like unwrapping a parcel. 'The Russian trains run on five feet, one-half inch tracks,' he went on, 'the European standard is four feet, eight and a half inch. Ergo, at the Russian border, we must change carriages. Wait – ' for Anna tried to interrupt – 'that's how it used to be. I know that with these new express trains, they simply hoist our carriages on narrower, I think bogies is the word. No difference; everyone, old or young, important or anonymous, has to get out. And, it takes at least an hour.'

'Oh.'

He wasn't put off by what seemed her lack of enthusiasm. 'Nothing,' he said with relish, 'no diplomatic passport, no ukase from the Czar, can save Undersecretary Draskovich from having to get out of his private compartment and into

25

the cold world. It is that three-and-a-half-inch difference between the railroad tracks of the Russian and the Austrian Empires that will be his undoing.'

'Four.'

'What?'

'Four inches,' Anna said. 'The difference in gauge is four inches.'

He stared at her. For the first time, he was really focusing on her face.

'I'm sorry,' she said. 'Don't let me spoil your story. You said, five and one-half, and four feet eight and a half.'

'Well, yes, right, four inches. Do you like the plan?'

'Why in Granitsa?' she asked. 'Why not in Petersburg, for instance, before he got on?'

'Oh, but in Petersburg he had a guard, there would have been a fight, we'd never have got away with it, or if we had, where could you take him? Granitsa is a mile from the border, Galicia, which is Polish, anti-Russian, anti-Austrian, anti-everybody. My friends got a farm there, or some kind of cabin, in the mountains.'

'What will you do with him?'

'We'll decide together,' he answered. 'I don't mean to be the boss. We may want him as a hostage for Sophia. Or maybe keeping him a while will be enough to frustrate the extradition.'

'Or maybe we should hang him for all his crimes. Or spread the word that he has defected from the service and is playing roulette in Monte Carlo with stolen state money . . . you know, he looks a bit like you, you could impersonate him.'

'Well, thank you,' Tolcheff said. He had now lost the last thread of pomposity. I'd start feeling sorry for him, she thought, but no doubt he'll gain it back.

'And what's my role in this?' she asked.

'It's crucial. To get him away from the other passengers. We must deliberate about it. I'll find out from my train friends what the set-up is when the train makes the change in gauge. But you see, don't you, the beauty of the plan is, if there's no struggle, if no one even notices. And that's your job. You want to be in on it, don't you?'

'Yes, indeed, I do,' Anna said. 'You can count on me, Andrew.'

They fell silent. The train started slowing down. 'Vilna,' he said, getting to his feet. 'I'll be back later.'

'What are you precisely,' she asked, 'to have all these contacts everywhere?'

He smiled.

'Now don't start looking mysterious and professorial again,' she said.

'I'll be back. Be careful now, keep your door closed.'

VII. From Vilna to the Niemen River

It had got warm in her compartment. She jumped down from her bed and opened the cupboard, which lowered the washbasin into place. Behind the mirror was a cabinet in which she found heavy white towels and a bar of French soap. She put one towel on the floor to stand on, took all her underclothes off, and started to soap herself. She was singing.

The train was running through a kind of hollow now, and on the rim the first houses of Vilna appeared, brick with wooden beams in the walls. They don't look very Russian any more, she thought, we're already entering the marches of this Empire. A path ran along the top, she saw a horse cart, and a bicyclist who for a moment tried to keep up with the train. She was naked but she didn't care, they were quite far off, and anyway, there was no link, the train made you untouchable, invulnerable. She hadn't seen herself in the nude for months, it was too cold for that in her Petersburg bedroom. I am a bit thin, she thought, patting her ribs, I've lost weight. Still, it's not bad, not bad at all. To hell with that swine Draskovich.

She took clean things out of her suitcase, this was a fresh day, new start. Slippers, I can't leave the compartment anyway. She kicked the black pumps far under the lower berth, she never wanted to see them again.

Then the heavy shadow of the station roof fell on the mirror and the train came to a halt. Now I'd better lower the blind, suppose Draskovich takes a stroll along the platform. But it was only a minute before the whistle sounded and they started to roll again, gently.

It's nice to be rich, she thought. She had been reminded for a second of a summer trip, years ago, a school excursion, all she remembered of it were the endless, excruciating halts in hot little stations, flies buzzing, the air totally still, and no visible reason why the wretched third-class train didn't move on. Money shields from the pain of living. The pains. Not the pain. God, this train is fast. I wonder when we'll be at the frontier.

She tried to visualise the map; there was Warsaw first, and then still quite a chunk of land.

'The General Government of Poland, integral part of Russia, contains fifty thousand square miles.' That was from the fourth-grade geography book. Not much help. Andrew Tolcheff would know.

She dressed carefully, brushed her reddish brown hair back and tied it with a ribbon. Of a sudden, she chased for her pocket-book and dug out the passport, to see what colour hair it gave for Tolcheff's sister. 'Dark brown.' She hadn't noticed that before. I could have dyed mine. It doesn't matter, women mess around with their hair colour. The eyes were right: grey. The inspector in Petersburg had hardly opened the thing.

A knock on the door, not Andrew's. 'What is it?' she called out.

'The attendant, madam. Do you want me to make the bed and close up the berths?'

She opened the door. 'Eh, yes. I feel a bit better.'

Then she sat by her window, looking out over pine groves amidst fields, with patches of snow only, black ploughed earth, and rows of birches. Flights of crows.

A wide curve brought the train into a valley, and then it got on to a viaduct; she could see the stone arches ahead, and deep down, very far below her, a river, dark blue glittering water, not even frozen. We're going south.

VIII. From the Niemen to Bialystok

Tolcheff was facing her, deadly pale. He's one of those who don't look older when they're worried, she thought. More like a sick child. 'What happened?' she asked him.

But he just sat there shaking his head and muttering to himself. All she heard was, 'stupid bastard'. 'Myself, I mean,' he finally said. 'You know what?'

She waited.

'I've made an unforgivable mistake.'

She was tempted to say, 'You?' but he seemed too miserable for irony.

He swallowed hard. 'We don't change gauge at the border. It is done – in Warsaw! For some incredible reason this bloody government built narrow-gauge railroad tracks from the Austrian border to Warsaw! Can you believe it? If you'd suggest that Poland may not be quite quite part of the Holy Russian Empire, the Czar'd have a fit and they'd haul you off to jail so fast you won't be able to button up your pants, but nevertheless, some damn official, some bureaucrat, decided for some reason that we'd have West European railroad gauge from the border to Warsaw.'

'Didn't your friends know?'

'Yes. Of course they did. They just told me. But I had

never told them what this was about, they wouldn't want any part of it; all they know is that they're giving me a free ride to the border. The other crew close their eyes to it, they get their turn for their friends. You see, there's nothing political about it. God, they'd piss in their pants.'

'Your language has become less professorial, too,' Anna said, but he paid no attention.

'Those two men who'll be at the border,' he said. 'They're all right, of course. But I couldn't tell them either, all they know is, to be there. Between Granitsa, and Szczakova across the frontier, passports and luggage are checked *on the train*. It will be midnight then. Draskovich will be sitting in his goddamn compartment with his feet up, and the inspectors will give him a respectful little bow from the door and move on.'

He took a deep breath. 'I'm sorry. Let's look the situation in the eye, and make another plan.'

'Maybe you should tell me a bit more about yourself,' Anna said. 'I'm in the dark about the whole business.'

'I know rail union people, I've worked for them. They're semi-illegal, but they're strong. Railroad men, and printers, they're always the strongest unions. So they give me free rides. I have this uniform, and I help in the mail van, things like that – not on this train, it doesn't carry mail.'

'I understand. You told me. But those two men at the border. Those ins of yours at the Ministry.'

He hesitated. 'I'm an organiser for the Second International.'

As she stared at him without speaking, he started explaining, 'The Socialist International which – '

'Yes, yes,' she said. 'But well, dammit, Tolcheff.'

A silence.

Then Anna shrugged. 'Oh well, I may as well be hanged for a sheep as for a lamb. You bastard, you could have warned me.'

'I'm sorry, Ann,' he muttered. 'I thought, the less you knew, the safer for you.'

'Hmm.'

'No one knows, you see. But now you understand why I – Michael was arrested in my place. We figured they'd have to let him go, there was no proof, nothing. But they killed him, I'm sure of it.'

'So let's get Draskovich,' she said slowly.

The colour had come back to his face. 'Did you love Michael?'

'No. Not in the sense you mean.'

'Of course Warsaw would have been just the perfect place to pull something this side of the border. And – I – did – not – know. And sent my two Warsaw contacts in great haste to Granitsa. Can you believe it?'

She only sighed.

'All right,' Tolcheff said. 'Well, first of all, we must keep on his tail. There'll be another chance. We'll create another chance. You have your ticket to Cannes, and a passport. I have neither, of course.'

'Why did you buy me a ticket all the way to Cannes, anyway?'

'It was safer. They ask no questions for France. If you go to Vienna, let alone Granitsa, there are papers and formalities. I'll get myself my ticket and passport in Warsaw. It's the only way to stay on. My train pals definitely won't smuggle me across the border.'

'How long is the Warsaw stop?'

He pulled out a little notebook. 'We get in at 5.36 this afternoon. . . . The Warsaw stop, Ann, is one hour and twenty minutes. And that includes shunting from Praga Station to Vienna Station.'

'And a dramatic four-inch change in gauge,' she couldn't resist adding. But he looked so pained that she said, 'Come on, Andrew. Don't lose your sense of humour. The Second International is watching you.'

He smiled half-heartedly. 'What do you know about us?' he asked.

'Oh, I've read about the First International, and Marx and Bakunin, and all that.'

'Well, a lot has happened since then. We were founded in

1889, a hundred years after the French Revolution, and by now every socialist party has joined.'

'I'm through with all that stuff,' she said.

'You are? Through with it, at the age of . . . ?'

'Twenty-five. Never mind that. Let's think about Warsaw.'

'You must let me tell you about Bakunin one day.'

'All right,' she said. 'You're not really a Russian, are you?'

'I was born in Petersburg, they think of me as Russian. I've never applied for a single document. The less they have in their files on you, the better. My brother-in-law says my English is without accent. Or less accent than half the Americans he knows. He thinks if I pursued it, I could claim American citizenship.'

'But not today in Warsaw at 5.36 p.m.'

He began to laugh. 'You're very calm and collected about it all. I'll pull myself together. And I apologise.'

As she didn't answer, he went on, 'For being self-important, and for not realising that you . . .' He didn't know how to go on.

'Tell me,' Anna asked after a moment, 'why do you bother with all this? If your father wasn't Russian, why not leave this whole mess behind? Why fight our fights?'

He looked offended. 'It's not your fight, it's everyone's fight. It's a world-wide lifelong fight. The mess is the same everywhere, it just shows more in some countries than in others. I'm not a Russian patriot or any kind of patriot. I think "international" is the most beautiful word in any language. The *Internationale* is the most beautiful anthem in the world, the only one without bombs or kings or God as the commander-in-chief of the army. Have you ever heard it?'

'No. I don't think it's played regularly in Petersburg.'

He laughed again. 'I'll bring you something to eat.'

IX. Bialystok-Warsaw

The train was running now amidst thick forest. It seemed to go even faster because the wall of trees was so close to the windows. A pale, low winter sun had come through the clouds and was just grazing the glass.

They had bread, two apples, and tea from an enamel container. 'It's all I could find to steal in the van,' he told her. 'It's going to be tricky later.'

'You know what has always seemed the summit of luxury to me? Eating in the restaurant car of a train. I remember wondering as a little child how they could put food on tables that were going by so fast.'

'I'll arrange it. On this train or another one. I promise you,' Tolcheff said.

'Will you? I'll have madrilène, a grilled turbot please with green beans, and then a tournedos and those small round potatoes.'

'With a magnum of Nuits Saint Georges.'

'A what?'

'Nuits Saint Georges, the wine? I'm not interested in that kind of thing,' he assured her, 'it's that mysterious name, nights of Saint George, that's what made me always remember it.' He thought he needed to explain himself further. 'Stephen told me about it. The Ambassador's vintage 1892 Nuits Saint Georges, the greatest diplomatic asset of the American Embassy, he says. Stephen is my brother-in-law. He likes to go on about topics like that.'

'I haven't been a Foreign Service daughter for a long time now,' Anna said as if in answer. 'I've earned my keep since I was sixteen. I did housework at the seminary, before they gave me a scholarship. For a very long year and a half.'

'But your father?'

'Oh – he's retired. He goes for walks along the Nevski with his new wife, in spats, he thinks he's a Paris boulevardier. I could have squeezed an allowance out of him but it was too much hard work. It was easier to scrub the kitchen in the seminary. I'm a working woman,' she said with a solemnity he didn't know whether to take seriously or not, 'and don't you fellows of the Second International forget it.'

There was a slight curve in the roadbed, and the sun for one second brightly lit her face.

She caught the expression with which he looked at her. 'It was terribly cold in my berth last night,' she said, 'my feet were like lumps of ice.'

He reddened.

'There was probably something wrong with the steam heat,' she added, 'but I thought I'd better not complain and draw attention.'

Tolcheff seemed at a loss for an answer. 'I'll go back to the van now,' he finally said, 'and get ready for Warsaw.'

'You think you'll manage everything in time?'

'Yes. Do you think I could borrow your twenty roubles?'

When he had gone, she tucked her feet in under her, and turned to the window, with her head against the velvet of the back.

Tolcheff had vanished from her mind.

She tried to penetrate the forest with the intensity of her looking, it was as if there were a straight clearing running from her eyes into the depths of the trees, turning like the spoke of a wheel, then disappearing while a new one was formed, one after the other. She couldn't see the sun, almost touching the horizon, because the train was now going straight into it, but very long shadows formed and unformed alongside the track, and a cold red light wavered between the bare branches.

She shook her head. I'm hypnotising myself. I'm in an undertaking of high politics, or low politics, or criminal politics, whatever it is, but I'm not serious, I'm sinking again

34

into some kind of dream. This is crazy, I, the hard-boiled, practical, whatever they always call me. It must be the motion. Or just the journey, the vacuum of a journey.

She giggled. She had suddenly thought of her father in those spats of his, eating his morning pastry at Filippov's, what he'd say if he could see his daughter speeding through Russian Poland with a stolen passport.

But the reality of it was quite peaceful.

She didn't stir until it had got dark in her compartment, until the last late light had vanished from under the trees. I wish this train would go on forever, she thought.

X. Warsaw (arrival)

Tolcheff jumped to the platform before the express had come to a stop. It was 5.37 on the station clock. A minute late, too, damn it. He didn't dare run, but he walked through a service door and out as fast as he could. Then he stood still in the station square, bewildered by the darkness and the almost deserted streets in front of him.

There was a two-horse cab, a neat thing with rubber tyres, standing under a lamp-post, and he asked the driver, in his very bad Polish, why everything was so quiet.

The man shrugged and gave him a cold stare. 'This is Praga. You're on the right bank.'

'How long does it take you to get me to the centre of town?'

'I go fast,' the driver said. 'But it costs a rouble.'

'All right. Please hurry. And stop by a police station on the way.'

They crossed on an endlessly long iron bridge. In front of them, the town came down to the river with a thousand lights blinking against the dark sky, walled to the right by a stone mass with a solitary lamp or two, the citadel. Power. The prison. But I enter under your guns.

They came to an abrupt stop at a grey building on the corner of the quay. 'The police,' the driver said.

Tolcheff ran in and asked the man at the desk, 'Where's the American consulate?'

'Aleja Ujazdovska. Number 18. But they're closed now. What do you need?'

He had already run out again.

The traffic on the quay was slow, carts with lumber and with barrels. Don't let it be far, he prayed. But then they turned into a side street and stopped.

'You sure this is it?' A nondescript little house.

'Yes.'

'Please wait for me.'

He pulled the bell. Tortuously slow steps, and then a manservant in uniform opened the door and stared at Tolcheff in his grey Russian railroad coat.

'Yes, yes, I lost my luggage,' Tolcheff said to him in English. 'I must see the consul. Urgently.'

The servant pointed to the brass doorplate, which said, 'Hours 10–3.'

'Never mind that,' Tolcheff said, 'it's an emergency.'

The man shook his head and pointed once more at the numeral 3.

'Oh damn. Don't you understand? Urgent. Important. That's what the consul is for. He is a public servant.' He got himself worked up as if he were really an American tourist in adversity.

The servant shook his head again. 'Consul is out,' he said at last.

'Well, I'll wait,' Tolcheff answered, and squeezing past him, opened an office door behind which he saw light and went in. The office was empty.

'Wait, stop,' the man shrieked. 'Come out.'

'My passport must be here,' Tolcheff improvised. 'The consul promised. Just let me look for it.' And he tried to open a drawer which, however, was locked.

'Come out or I call police.'

'Just a second,' Tolcheff said, trying another drawer. The servant hurried out of the room and Tolcheff heard him turn the crank of a telephone in the corridor and then start shouting.

'Fuck it,' he muttered. He looked around once more, tried a filing cabinet, locked, too; then he saw a twenty-five-rouble note, tucked under the edge of the office typewriter. He pulled it out and put it in his pocket.

He came into the corridor, where the man dropped the receiver and now tried to prevent him from leaving. Tolcheff pushed him aside, got out, and slammed the door behind him. The cab, with its nervous horses, had moved some way beyond the door, and he was in it before the servant had reappeared in view.

He leaned back when they had rounded the corner. That wasn't too good. I should have said – Twenty-five roubles, though.

'Where to now?' the driver called.

'Just keep going for a moment.'

They entered a wide, animated avenue, with shops and cafés, cast-iron lamp-posts with dazzling gaslight, throngs of pedestrians, not as cold, noisier than Petersburg. There were Christmas decorations in the shopwindows, packed bakeries, flowers. He looked at a man and a woman in the flower shop, he could see through the steamed-over window that they were laughing; he felt a pang of envy, people going home to warm December living rooms. He shook that off, they're like cows, they don't know about the great world-wide battle – My second plan.

'Do you know where Karolkowa Droga is?' he asked the driver. He had had to check the name in his notebook, he could never remember it. It was the street where his contacts lived, both the men he had asked to go to Granitsa. There might be a relative there, a father or a wife who would at least lend him a suit and money. The cab driver stopped his horses and pulled a grubby street guide out of his coat pocket. Tolcheff groaned.

'I'm not sure,' the driver finally told him. 'Somewhere in the south-western district.'

'Far?'

'An hour.'

Tolcheff shook his head. 'Very well then,' he said, 'in that case I need a shopping street. But not this one. A cheaper one. Do you understand me? A poorer one.'

The driver frowned and turned the first corner at full speed, rattled across a square with empty market stalls, and finally stopped at the beginning of a narrow, bustling alley-way.

'Cheap enough?' he asked without a smile. 'Shops of Jews.'

'Fine. Wait for me here, please.'

'I can't wait. How do I know you'll be back? It's three roubles.'

'Oh damn you,' Tolcheff cried. He had tears of frustration in his eyes as he rummaged through the small notes Anna had given him. 'Here, three roubles. Three more when I come back. All right?'

'All right.'

XI. Warsaw (departure)

Twenty roubles bought Tolcheff a third-hand dinner jacket, trousers, evening shoes, a shirt that was too wide at the neck, and a butterfly tie. Even in the bad light of the tailor's shop, the material looked shiny and threadbare, but he had no time to bargain. He kept it all on, with his coat over it and the uniform in a parcel. The cab driver glanced at the black shoes and trousers sticking out from under the railroad coat, but didn't show any further interest.

'What's the best hotel?' Tolcheff asked him.

'The Europa.'

'To the Europa, please.'

Luck was now with him, Tolcheff thought; he could see through the wide glass doors that there was a travel agency in the lobby, with coloured posters of mountains and very blue lakes. He slipped out of his coat. 'Pull up a bit farther,' he said, 'and wait.' He had another three-rouble note ready this time.

He walked back along the sidewalk into the hotel, entered the restaurant, came out again, and went to the travel counter. There was no one in sight and he knocked on the glass.

Twenty-eight minutes past six.

A girl appeared.

'Please make out a first-class ticket to Cannes for me,' he said, trying to speak unhurriedly. 'With the express surcharge.'

'Cannes, France, sir?'

'No, Cannes, China!' Tolcheff cried.

The girl stared at him.

'Excuse me, yes, France,' he said. 'For – ' He was on the verge of saying, 'tonight,' but swallowed the word just in time. 'For today a week. The special train.'

She filled out a coupon, looked up things, stamped the coupon. 'Upper berth or lower berth, or private?' she asked.

'Lower.'

'What name, sir?'

'Draskovich.' It was the only name that came to his mind. 'Come on, dear. I have to go to the theatre.'

'I'm sorry, sir,' she answered indignantly. 'You don't want me to make a mistake.'

'No, no, of course not.'

She put all the documents in an envelope and handed it to him.

'It adds up,' she said, consulting her pad, 'to a hundred and eighteen roubles, and fifty kopek.'

'Put it on my bill,' Tolcheff said. 'Room 207. And this is for you.' He dropped a ten-rouble bill on the counter, and ran out.

'Sir,' the girl cried, but he was already back in his cab. 'Vienna Station,' he shouted.

The coachman didn't move.

Vision of the girl running after him. The doorman pulling him out of his cab. Ann on the train, alone.

'What's the matter?' he asked furiously.

'I didn't understand, sir.'

'The station for Vienna – Wiedenski.'

The cab rolled off. He struggled back into his coat. He was afraid to look back.

When they pulled up at Vienna Station, it was ten to seven. I've made it, he told himself. The train was due to leave at 6.57.

His cab driver said something he didn't understand, and he handed him one more rouble. 'I'm on your side, you know,' he told him, 'even if I speak the language of your oppressors.'

The driver gave him a dirty look and tore off.

'Well, screw you, too,' Tolcheff called after him. A group of railroad workers was going into the station, and he hastily followed them, but a policeman was guarding the service entrance and they all showed some kind of pass.

He turned and marched into the main entrance, taking off his coat again. Dammit, I left my parcel in the cab.

His train was posted at the top of the board, 'D-Express with surcharge. Vienna Nord, Vienna Sud, Udine, Venice, Milan, San Remo. Monte Carlo, Cannes. Platform 1.'

Right in front of him. It was standing there, the engine facing him, gleaming, different from ordinary engines on ordinary trains, haughtily blowing clouds of very white and clean steam.

He'd go to the news-stand, get papers and cigarettes to look more – no, nonsense, no histrionics. He dropped his overcoat on a bench and walked to the platform gate.

The ticket inspector took in Tolcheff's dinner jacket, went

painstakingly through the papers in the envelope, and then asked, 'And your luggage receipts, sir?'

'Oh – My luggage is already on the train. Everything is. My passport, too. I came on this train from Saint Petersburg. I was only booked to Warsaw, but I changed my mind.'

The man seemed unhappy and turned his head as if looking for someone to advise him, then went through all the coupons and receipts once more, down to an advertisement for a circus the girl had put in, which he studied, too.

'I met a lady on the train,' Tolcheff said with a terrible smirk. 'We decided to travel on together.'

The ticket man did not appear amused by this.

'Come on,' Tolcheff said, 'it's five to seven. Here, for your trouble.'

And he gave him the little ball of rouble notes he had left in his pocket. Oh God, he thought that same instant, a terrible mistake, railroad employees are incorruptible.

But the ticket inspector wasn't. 'This has to be regularised on the train,' he said. 'You cannot cross the border if you do not – '

As he had pocketed the money, there seemed no need to listen to him further. 'Yes, I'll see to it,' Tolcheff interrupted, pulled the envelope out of the man's hand, and climbed aboard the first carriage.

XII. Warsaw-Piotrkov

He slumped down and dramatically wiped his forehead. Anna started to laugh.

'Don't tell,' she said, 'I know. You've got yourself hired in the train string quartet.'

'What? Oh that.' Then he smiled back at her and stood up to look at himself in the mirror. 'Well, it got me on the train anyway. I had tried on a business suit first, which was worse. Evening clothes make people less suspicious of you.'

'Not if that cuff falls off,' Anna said. 'It's about to.'

'It can't be that bad. The train conductor was very polite.'

'What happened?'

'Well, first of all my reservation was for next week. I had done that on purpose, or the girl – never mind that. I told the conductor the travel agency must have made a mistake. No problem, he said, I'll give you a nice compartment all to yourself. No, I'm going to join a friend, I said. Then, my heavy luggage was all shipped ahead, I said, and how I liked to travel light, and he said, yes, he'd once known a gentleman who only carried a toothbrush, and I said this and he said that, and then I said I'd take good care of him at the end of the journey.'

'How much money did you raise? How much have we left now?'

'Nothing.'

'Nothing!'

'What do you think? First I had to buy this suit, and actually – '

'Say no more!' Anna cried. 'It was well worth it.'

'Please don't start laughing again. And I still don't have a passport.'

'Oh damn.' After a moment she said, 'I'm new to this, but it seems to me that we're working ourselves sick just trying to stay on this train ... while Draskovich is drinking his bottles of Nuits Saint Georges in the diner without a worry in his head.'

'I'm new to it, too. Union organising was never like this.'

'Your train friends must begin to wonder about you. I mean you sitting here for hours, and now this outfit, and all that.'

'They think it's all part of an affair I'm having with a married woman.'

'Me?'

'Yes.' He stared at his shoes and then gave her a quick glance, but she just nodded, 'Good. You haven't asked what happened here,' she said.

'What happened?'

'A lot of commotion. Disconcerting. But for the track change, this carriage had come to a stop almost right in front of a ladies' room. I ran in and stayed in, through all the banging and the announcements, till the third departure bell. I didn't see a soul.

'And I had to walk through the whole train. You see, it had entered Vienna Station headfirst. I was lucky, the corridor was on the off side, everyone was at the other windows, looking out on to the platform. People dress for dinner on this train and I wasn't a bit conspicuous like this.'

'Were the women elegant?'

'Rich old biddies. But I saw Draskovich.'

'Oh . . .'

'It was all right. I was very careful, he couldn't possibly have seen me. He was reading, and drinking some kind of apéritif, I think.'

'A cat and mouse game,' Anna announced, nodding her head. 'With two mice in pursuit of a happy fat cat.'

'Don't you worry, there'll be a change of roles. I promise you. We have to cross the border first.'

The inky darkness outside was broken first by lines and flashes of light, and then the train raced without slowing down through a brightly lit station.

'Skiernievice,' he said. 'God, we're flying.'

'How far from the border are we?'

'A hundred and fifty miles.'

'Do you know what to do?'

'Those two contact men,' he told her. 'One's about my age, dark, too, his name is Jan. The other is much younger, blondish, he looks like a boy. He's called – never mind that. I thought if you'd get out at Granitsa, for a stroll on the platform sort of. It'll be very cold, and you can hide yourself in a scarf up to your ears. You're bound to notice them. Tell them there's been a mistake. Ask Jan to give you his passport for me. I think that's the way out.'

'Why would he trust me?'

'Who else would know of him there, if it weren't through me?'

She thought a moment. 'All right, I'll try. Where will you be?'

'Out of sight somewhere. But not in such a way that I'm obviously hiding and up to no good.'

'Creep in my bed,' she suggested. 'You're pretty thin, maybe they won't even notice you.'

He smiled hesitantly. 'But you'll be right back with the passport.'

'If he gives it.'

'He will, we've got real solidarity.'

XIII. Piotrkov-Granitsa

A long, unbroken wall of yellowish stone appeared, just barely visible in the shimmer from the compartment lights which accompanied the train; then a street lamp showed a paved road parallel to it. The train went through an unlit tunnel, and emerging, picked up the road once more. The presence of a little town out there in the dark was betrayed by a rare gaslight, silhouetting low-roofed houses. Not a window was lit. The train had slowed down as if afraid to shatter those old structures.

Then it gathered new speed. The last street lamp showed that the cobbles had come to an end and the road changed to sand and mud, and all outside was blackness again. She shivered.

'Piotrkov,' Tolcheff murmured.

'What?'

'That was Piotrkov.'

'Oh. Doesn't anyone live in Piotrkov? Have the inhabitants fled on the news of our arrival?'

I've made a mess of things, he thought, and she's fed up. 'These are poor towns,' he answered her, 'towns in the Warta marshes, forgotten corners of Europe, old battlefields, and nothing since . . . these people have no money to burn oil lamps, they go to bed when it's dark.'

'I'm cold and hungry,' she said. 'Let's not sit here any longer like this. I'm going to creep into bed too.'

She took off her dress and her slippers, climbed up on to her berth and got under the blankets. 'You can come up here,' she said. 'No, don't lock the door.'

'Why not?'

'I've an idea.'

He fussed around a while, and finally took off his jacket and shoes and lay down beside her, on top of the cover. She pulled the blankets out from under and put them over him. 'Warm me,' she said. 'Don't worry, I'm just a political accomplice.'

'You're . . .' He wanted to say something flattering, but he couldn't think of anything that didn't sound lame.

There was a knock on the door, and he jumped, but she held him down. 'Stay where you are.'

An attendant came in and began automatically, 'I've come to make the bed, madam,' then saw their heads sticking out, coughed, turned around, and banged the door shut behind him.

Anna laughed.

'What are you doing?' Tolcheff asked nervously. 'Why was that? You must be crazy.'

'I'm establishing your place here. Building up a kind of alibi for you in here in case your friend refuses.'

'He – Apologies, Ann. Apologies once more. I'll shut up. You are very much better at all this than I am.'

'Just make warmth,' she said.

She turned her back against him. She liked the feeling of his body pressed close, in an impersonal, totally chaste way;

she felt her thoughts about what had to be done become vague again, the motion of the train and its sounds renewed their hold on her. I better leave the light on, she thought, we can't risk falling asleep. The blind was up, but the window reflected the compartment only, she couldn't see herself or him, it was as if it were empty. She tried to visualise her own movement, horizontal, sideways, speeded across the Polish plain, those sombre marshes that seemed abandoned by all life. Skeletons in armour, in rotting leather, soldiers killed centuries ago sinking down and down into the mud, a strange idea, a sideways hurtling over them, reverberations of a twentieth-century train echoing down into their depth —

She realised she had been asleep, she didn't know how long. What had awakened her was his carefully turning away from her.

She moved her hand and it bumped against his body, and she felt that he was very excited. It didn't excite her, but it moved her. Suddenly and strangely her last resentment at his past overbearing manner vanished, and she felt sorry for him. Sorry for this thin fellow, already nearing middle age, full of an undirected love no one seemed to want particularly, working for a revolution that wouldn't happen or surely not in his lifetime.

What pathetic creatures we all are, she thought. How brief it all is.

Lying on her back, she wriggled out of her underskirt and her panties, then turned and kissed him.

XIV. Granitsa

It was seventeen minutes past midnight, Petersburg time, when the train pulled into Granitsa. Anna was standing at the carriage door, wrapped up in two scarves. 'Ten-minute stop only, madam,' a conductor warned her. 'Customs inspection will be on the train. Do you have your passport?'

She held it up. 'I just need some air, I don't feel so well.'

As she stepped down, she swayed with tiredness, and the cold gritty wind blowing across the cement platform made tears run down her cheeks. Railroad employees or customs men in uniform were standing around in a small group. Through a plate-glass window she saw a buffet with a waitress and a yawning man leaning over the counter, but there seemed to be no passengers getting on or off.

'Damn you, Tolcheff,' she said through her teeth, which made her feel better. She walked away from the white arc light, and then, in the shadow of a loaded freight cart, she saw two people sitting on crates. They were wearing fur caps and scarves, impossible to see their hair colour or even their faces. But she stopped in front of the tallest one and said, 'Good evening, Jan.'

The man jumped up and stared at her.

'You're Jan?'

'Yes. Who are you?'

'A friend of Andrew's. Things are in a mess. He's on the train, he can't get off, he has no passport. He wants you to lend him yours.'

'What's going on?' the other man asked in broken Russian, and the two had an exchange in Polish.

'You better hurry,' Anna said, 'they're already starting the

47

inspection on the train.'

Jan stood silently shaking his head. 'One of Andrew's schemes,' he said bitterly to her. 'I'm not surprised.'

'He means well,' Anna said and smiled at him. 'My God, it's cold here.'

'But he made us both come to this place,' Jan said. 'We've travelled a whole day, we took the risk of entering a border zone – well, but fuck it. I beg your pardon.'

'Quite all right,' Anna said. 'Will you lend him your passport, though?'

He slowly shook his head.

She tried to go on smiling in the wind that pulled at her mouth. 'I understand you don't know me, but you must admit no policeman would dress up in a rabbit fur, accost you, and – '

'It's not that, we trust you. It's all familiar Andrew stuff. The point is, I have no passport.'

'What? How would we have got into Galicia then?'

'You must be joking – we cross over the mountains.'

They stared at each other, Anna stamping her feet to feel less cold. The younger man got a translation of the dialogue.

'Get him off the train,' Jan suggested. 'We'll get him across.'

'How could he get back on in time?'

'Hell, no. If that's what he wants, we can't help him.'

'Can you let us have some money?' she asked.

He pushed coins and a note into her hand. 'We'll wait near the music stand outside,' he said. 'Tell him to get off. He's risking his neck otherwise. And yours, maybe. You can't hide on these trains.'

She was back on at the second bell, blue with cold. She had seen inspectors move through the corridor, four or five carriages ahead from hers.

As she turned on the light in her compartment, Tolcheff came out from under her bed cover and climbed down. 'No passport,' she said, trying to catch her breath. 'They'll help you get away, they say you won't make it.'

48

He stood staring at her, then he shook his head. He had put his suit back on. She thought, he looks indeed like a down-on-his-luck violinist, like that poor guy that plays in the Donon café –

XV. Granitsa-Szczakova

There was a metallic tap on her door and the border police inspector came in, his rubber stamp in his hand and a little ink pad dangling from his belt. He was followed by a train conductor.

Anna was in her berth, her fur and various clothes draped over her feet. 'I was very cold,' she said with a weak smile. 'I've a touch of influenza, I think.' Tolcheff was under the blankets and all those articles of clothing, folded almost double, motionless.

The conductor was concerned. 'But you should have complained, madam. Your radiator isn't functioning properly.'

She had put her case open on the lower berth, the passport and her ticket beside it. 'It's all there,' she pointed.

The inspection was summary but the two men stayed in the doorway, going over a list. Hers was the last compartment, and they seemed hesitant. Then they said, 'Madam,' saluted, and left.

Tolcheff did not stir, but he made an air hole towards the wall, and she heard him take deep breaths. 'They're still out there,' she whispered.

'They've a name left unchecked on the list,' he whispered back.

'Yours.'

'My reservation is in the name Draskovich.'

She could hear the men speaking to each other, and then, she thought, another voice, and then laughter.

'Was that the toothbrush conductor?' she whispered.

'What?'

'Goddammit,' she said between her teeth. 'Was that the conductor with the chitchat about light travelling, the man who saw you on to the train?'

'Oh . . . I don't know, I couldn't hear his voice very clearly.'

A new tap on the door, and the conductor put his head in. From the corridor she could still hear laughter, malicious laughter, she thought.

Now, for the first time, she felt real panic. She began to tremble.

'I'll send the attendant to look at the heating, madam,' he said.

'Thank you. . . . No, tomorrow morning, please.' And she turned off the light before he had even closed the door again.

She lay still for a moment, then she bent down and murmured, 'You have more luck than you deserve, Tolcheff. But that was clever of you, that name. Two times Draskovich on the list, they may have thought it was a mistake. I wonder, though.'

'I didn't plan it. It was the only name I could think of, at the travel agency.'

'Maybe they knew you were in my bed. Maybe they thought they were saving some married lady from disgrace. I wonder.'

Steps of men, walking away. Anna bolted the door, and he crept out and lowered himself to the floor.

'Ann – ' he began.

'Just leave me alone for a moment,' she said in a strangled voice. 'It's all been a bit much.'

He kneeled at the window, his elbows on the sill, and looked out at the dark world flying by. Cupping his hand around his face, he could distinguish silhouettes of pine trees, hills, against a sky which had collected a touch of light from somewhere, from an invisible moon. At times the valley narrowed and the squares of light from the train windows were delineated on the slope, running alongside with them.

They crossed a deserted country road, sand, a lighter ribbon in the black night. Then dark oblong shapes of unlit buildings.

An empty, walled courtyard he could look down into. A row of wooden huts; a gate with an electric lamp and a guard post, painted black and yellow. It flashed by, and it took him a moment to realise what he had seen.

'Ann!' he cried. 'Barracks – the Habsburg colours! We're in Austria, we made it.'

'Hurrah,' she said.

'Aren't you pleased?'

'Yes.'

He did a kind of dance step. 'Can I come back?'

She hesitated. 'It's a very narrow bed. For a while.'

He took his clothes off, with his back towards her, and she looked at him in the bluish light of the night lamp.

'Are you afraid of me?' she finally asked.

'Eh – yes.'

He traced the slight rounding of her breasts with his fingers, through her nightgown, then he crept on top of her, a bony, cold body.

'God, you're cold,' she said.

He muttered, 'I'm sorry,' as he came into her.

She could feel his heart beat, very fast.

Then he whispered, 'Ann, can I let go?' and she nodded with her face against his.

'You were a bit late asking that,' she said after a while. 'What about our baby we made at the other side of the border, our Polish baby?'

'What?'

'Just a joke . . . I hope. You must get into the lower berth now. But don't disarrange it.'

'Ann,' he asked, 'do you like – ' He was going to say, 'Do you like me?' but changed it to, 'Did you like it?'

She gave a soft laugh. 'Yes,' she then said.

She heard him fumble around for a long time, she wondered what he was doing but kept her head under the cover. Then, when all had become quiet, she pushed the cover back and lay staring at the ceiling.

She realised she felt pleased with herself. I have got tough, and really so. It's not a pose.

They won't hurt me again. Not easily. Not likely.

Clinging together, just because, because you live in the same time span.

Of a sudden, she was terrified by the idea which those words conjured up, of time without end, flowing forward and backward, of clinging to who passed next to you like wreckage in a flood. But it was a panic of a second only. She giggled soundlessly. It surely helps to be in the same time span. Unless you're an Egyptologist, making love to a mummy.

XVI. Szczakova-Vienna Nord

She opened her eyes as the train was rolling through a built-up area. From her pillow she could see the sombre high walls of a factory complex, rows of dark windows, many cracked, with here and there a lamp burning deep in the interior although it was morning.

Tolcheff, dressed, his hair wetted down, but unshaven, was standing at the window. He turned towards her and said with a kind of soft intensity, 'Good morning, Ann.'

'Good morning.'

A silence.

'We just passed Wagram,' he said.

'Oh, Wagram! I'd have liked to see that. I think I like

Napoleon. Or perhaps I don't.'

'There was nothing to see. We'll be in Vienna in a few minutes. We've more than an hour there, and I'll be off, on an errand. I've got things under control now. You'll see. Here's five roubles from Jan's money.'

'How much was it?'

'Twenty-one roubles. Lots of it in kopeks. Poor devil. I'll pay him back.'

'What's this for?' she asked.

'As soon as I've gone, you must order yourself an enormous breakfast, here in the compartment.'

The train was slowing down and she sat upright. 'There's snow on the ground! God, you'll be cold. Don't you have a coat?'

'No. I went to the service van to get my bag and maybe borrow one, but the connecting door is locked. And there's a new crew, anyway. My overcoat is still in Warsaw.'

'You're pretty conspicuous.'

'Don't you worry.'

He unbolted the door, peeked around it, and was gone.

Anna got to the floor, scratched her head, studied her tongue in the mirror, and with her fur coat on over her nightgown, looked out.

An evenly slate-coloured sky hung low over fields without end. On a knoll behind willows sat a little castle, fat and round. Very unknightly.

The train turned, and in the curve she could see a long bridge. The embankment crossed a swampy wasteland, no snow there; then the cadence of the bridge girders began so abruptly that it made her jerk back her head.

So this is the Austrian Empire, and the Danube, the waltzes, the kitchenmaids with rosy cheeks seduced by the dashing officers in corsets, and the streets paved with the sweat and the blood of the subject races? Where did I read that? They exaggerate. Or maybe not. Empires, what a pretension. Fat shopkeepers, playing Roman warriors and robbing the world blind. A plague on them all.

They had crossed the bridge and turned sharply, running

above a street. She stuck her tongue out at a man and a woman staring at the train from a doorway, but they didn't see her, and then she was glad they hadn't. It was crowded there, throngs of people were marching below her, all men, carrying lunch boxes, in formation almost, entering double gates leading to a set of office buildings. They didn't look up at the train passing within a few feet of them, and when she looked back at their faces, she was struck by the visibility of their silence: not one of them seemed to be talking or even turning his eyes to a neighbour. Like a crowd in a dream, she thought. How strange that this is Vienna, that these are inhabitants of Vienna.

Think of that enormous distance, of Napoleon taking all those weeks or months to get through these vast countries. It is unnatural. I don't know where I am, this new century is destroying the mysteries of the world. Perhaps that is precisely what's needed to set us free. Different from what Tolcheff imagines.

They're weighing down on us, all those miles and centuries. There's a weight on each paving stone, each blade of grass, a thousand years of tired footsteps, and we'll get rid of it with machines, with trains.

On this train I'm free, and for the first time.

Except – she had a shiver of apprehension – that now we'll have to deal with Draskovich.

Deal with a man. God. Just dealing with a bee or a mouse, when you don't get them with the first blow, and they wriggle or try to crawl away and you have to go on batting them till they're still.

She felt half sick. With hunger, she thought. She climbed back in bed and pressed the bell for the car attendant.

XVII. Vienna

Tolcheff, after spending a rouble on a shave in the station, changed the remaining fifteen, for which they gave him thirty-five Austrian crowns. With these he entered a weapons shop on Prater Street off the station square.

In French, which he spoke reasonably well, he asked to be shown a small pistol.

'Monsieur is an officer?' the clerk asked.

'Indeed.' He waved at his dinner clothes with a little smile. 'Late party – haven't been home yet. I serve in a Hungarian unit.'

The clerk brought a velvet tray with several pistols, the cheapest of which cost thirty crowns.

'I'll take this one,' Tolcheff said, 'with a box of cartridges.'

The clerk thanked him with a little bow and said, 'If I may see your army paybook, sir.'

'Oh, I don't have it on me. Not in this suit, you see. I can drop by with it later if you want, tomorrow morning.'

'We'll have your parcel all ready for you. I have to hold it till then. Regulations, I'm afraid.'

Tolcheff tried to think of an answer. 'But I need it now,' he said. 'I need it today. It's for a photograph.' Pretty weak. He considered grabbing the thing and running out; but he was at the back, the shop was long and narrow. Several other people were between him and the door.

The clerk raised his eyebrows to indicate he was powerless.

'Well, damn, I never heard of such nonsense,' Tolcheff told him.

'I can let you have this one,' the clerk said, 'and it's only eighteen crowns.'

'Oh – why is that?'

'It's an alarm pistol, or a starter's pistol, if you will. It shoots blanks only. But in a photograph, as you said, it will look all right.'

'I'll take it,' Tolcheff answered and then felt obliged to add, 'I may come back with my army papers, to change it for one of those.' He pointed at the tray with the real pistols which the clerk had placed on a ledge behind him.

'If it hasn't been fired – ' the clerk began. 'But let me ask the manager.'

'No, no, don't bother. I'll keep this one also, anyway.'

'As you wish, sir. It makes a very fine bang.'

Damn you, a very fine bang indeed. I never took him in for a second. He figures I'm a night waiter in the station rather than a Hungarian officer. Good. I don't want to look like a Hungarian or any other officer. Oh, I don't know though. Don't Hungarian officers speak French, don't they go to all-night parties and walk home in the morning in their dinner jackets? Not walk home, saunter home. Is it something else, a lack of forcefulness in me, am I weak? Is that what makes me pedantic? Is that what Ann thinks? Is that why I didn't really excite her, or is she too shy to show it?

But she must have felt how much I wanted her, that soft curve of her breasts when you go upward with your hands, you feel her ribs, like a boy, and suddenly she is not at all like a boy, not at all, not at all. Her stomach, that flatness where her belly goes in. You can span her with one hand, you can feel yourself through her back – femininity – more than those fat breasts they always go on about. There is more manliness in wanting this thin girl . . . And isn't there more manliness in the work I do by myself and without anyone knowing, than in blustering about in a high collar, the puppet of some stupid government, state? Why do they have us on the defensive, why is that inane obedient thoughtlessness manly, why is patriotism the easy emotion and love for the people the tricky one?

He started to walk with a military step, looking the passersby sternly in the face. Captain Andrew Tolcheff of the First Imperial Hungarian Assault Battalion. Ready to kill.

But a delivery boy, coming out of a confectionery shop with a basket, did not step aside for him and they nearly bumped into each other. He looked in the mirror of the shop window and saw that the middle button of his jacket hung on a thread, almost coming off, and pulling it sideways.

That sight gave him a sudden pleasure. He stuffed the box with the pistol in his jacket pocket, which pulled it even more askew.

The people.

XVIII. Vienna Sud-Villach

'How did you make out?' she asked him.

'All right. I don't like the place. I spent a month in Vienna once.'

'Isn't it gay?'

'I guess so, in a beery sort of way. Beery – like beer? But I had a theory that it was just a myth, to keep the poor in check. We're okay, we're so *lustig*.'

'We're so what?'

'*Lustig*. A terrible word, no? Actually, they hate most everybody, they always had asides about "stupid foreigners" when they thought you couldn't understand.'

'You're not talking about the workers, I assume,' Anna said.

He smiled but did not answer.

'I'd been thinking I don't care for empires,' she went on, 'though all I've seen of this one are two stations and a park; and many people. They were very quiet, not, eh, lusty at all. Countries should be small. . . . You know, it is strange to see signs you can't read.'

A journey, out of my language. A voyage almost. 'How are we ever going to get back?' she asked.

'I have friends – ' He knew she'd smile at that and he made a face of, 'I can't help it. They'll wire me money. And no one asks to see your passport anywhere outside Russia either. We'll be fine.'

'You mean, this has the approval of your people?'

'Well, no . . . not officially. The Second International has a Brussels secretariat now, all very above board and proper. But in countries like Russia, and Austria, almost everything is forbidden and illegal, of course, and we have to be left alone and do what we think best.'

'And what do we think best?' she asked.

He had been waiting for that. He pulled the box out of his pocket and untied the string. As he carefully lifted off the lid, she thought for one crazy moment that he had bought a cake somehow connected with his Draskovich plot – to poison him? She giggled when he brought out the pistol, and he frowned at her.

He loaded it with four cartridges.

'Don't point at me,' she said. 'I don't like those things.'

'Actually – ' He was about to tell her of the clerk and what had happened in the shop, but then he decided against it. Damn it, he thought, am I now afraid to be laughed at? Didn't I always believe in the anti-hero?

'Right,' he said. 'Let me submit my plan to this special committee of two. Your job would be to get Draskovich to open his door. I'll come in right after you. Between Villach and Pontebba. At Pontebba, we will force him off the train, with this. From then on, it'll be the original Granitsa plan, but for a while it'll be just the two of us. Three, with the pistol.'

'Pontebba?'

'It's across the Italian border. You see, I have no contacts in this country, believe it or not. And the Austrians are a police state and they're everywhere, and they'd hand us over to the Russian police with great delight. I do have contacts in Italy. Specifically a boarding-house in – ' He looked in his notebook. 'I'm very bad at names, I sent them a telegram from Vienna, I thought it over very carefully – in Gamona, which is fifteen miles below the border, say twelve miles from Pontebba. They shelter Austrian deserters there, who come to them from Trieste. Pontebba is the place to get off, because it's the only stop near it, and it's wild country, too.'

'Will it really work? I mean, do you believe in it in your stomach, sort of?'

'Yes.'

'It sounds so wild. And I'm not very strong, you know.'

'I think you're very strong.'

'I mean,' she said, 'that I can't twist Draskovich's arms or any of that kind of thing. I've never even slapped anyone.'

'I – ' he began, and stopped.

'You start a lot of sentences,' she said, smiling, 'and don't finish them. Why is that?'

'I don't know. Perhaps because everything is relative, both one and the other, true and not true, black and not black.'

'That doesn't sound very revolutionary to me.'

'Oh, it's the conservatives who are the fanatics, not us,' he answered. 'You have to be a fanatic to maintain that this is a good world we've made.'

'Nature is good,' Anna said, pointing out through the window.

'Yes – What's that got to do with it?'

'Nothing,' she said lightly.

The train, after a long climb, was descending through pine forests covering very rough terrain, steep hillsides; she bent down low and looked up along the glass of the window, but still couldn't see the sky. Mountain streams cascaded down beside the track, and they crossed and recrossed a river on small viaducts. The light in the compartment went on and they entered a tunnel. The transition was so sudden that Anna uttered a cry.

He put his hand on hers. 'Don't be nervous.'

'But I am. Aren't you?'

'Yes. Do you accept the plan?'

'I guess so. If you believe in it, and you have that boarding-house, and all those contacts. . . . I'd have preferred at this point just to follow him to France, and go see Sophia, and take care he can't get her extradited.'

'But how?'

She thought. 'All right. Pontebba it is. Propaganda by the deed.'

After that they sat silently by the window looking out. It was a long afternoon. The train went through narrow valleys and through and around mountains; there were old castles everywhere, watchtowers and ruins. At times, when they were climbing, she felt as if the progress out of that country, that other Empire, was intolerably slow. Then again the train seemed to race, to eat up the time she wanted to hold on to. The last peaceful hours, she imagined. In Pontebba this peace and almost well-being will be over. Far though it is, it will be like being back home.

Once she said, 'It's such a wild, rocky landscape, so untamed. You wonder how the people can be so itsy-bitsy then, with their waltzes and their lusty – whatever that was.'

'I don't think it's really wild,' he answered. 'I can't imagine anyone getting killed in these mountains. It's all pictures for boxes of chocolates.'

'Now you're imposing some idea of yours upon it all. You'd be dead all right if you fell down that slope.' She pointed to a sheer rock wall. A few tiny pine trees grew out of it, from a small ledge covered with snow.

On that ledge it was already dark.

Then they didn't say another word and watched as the light faded from the compartment. Outside, the dark had a reddish tint to it and made it seem to her as if his eyes were glittering. The quiet of trees in the evening. Simplicity. Can't we get back to it without turning everything upside down first, is there really nothing between being a hermit on a pillar in the desert and going after Draskoviches on trains? It's Tolcheff who forces us into alternatives.

I'd better enjoy my in-between hour.

When she opened her pocketbook and pulled out her little watch, the chain of which had broken, he said, 'Don't look. It's all right, there is still plenty of time.'

XIX. Villach-Saifnitz

It was peculiar to walk through this train. She had become used to the idea that she couldn't leave her compartment, and to the sense of peace that gave her. All she had had so far of the express were the few feet of corridor from her door to the toilet. Now she was walking in the other direction, forward, past other compartments. She had her shoes back on and wore her coat, and she was carrying her pocketbook stuffed with some of her possessions, for she wouldn't get back. She looked to see if Tolcheff was right behind her, but he wasn't.

The train had been running for a long time through a narrow defile which had cut off the view of a sombre purple sunset. They emerged now and she went to a window to look, but the sky had grown dark everywhere. She had lost track of the date. Mid-December, they were nearing the shortest day; two nights on this train already. She passed through the two connecting doors into the next carriage.

Here several people were standing at the windows in the corridor. They stepped back to let her pass. Interested looks. She had to hold on to the gleaming brass rod along the wall as the train swayed. Voices, laughing, a steward in a white jacket with a tray with glasses. It was cocktail hour, with much coming and going. A different world. Andrew and I are like waifs really, we've got a nerve wanting to play a role here, in this world of all these fashionable, rich creatures, thinking we can make our will felt. The steward slid a compartment door open and entered sideways to give her more room to pass. 'Un soupçon de soda seulement, le soupçon d'un soupçon,' she heard a woman's voice. At that moment she felt closer to Tolcheff than when she was lying under him in the night.

The following carriage was a restaurant car, with a gangway leading to two sections of tables and chairs. People were having drinks, except for the tables in two corners which were already laid with white tablecloths and where children were eating their dinners, a girl in one corner with her mother, two at the other with a nanny in a white and blue uniform. As she looked at them, a waiter came up and asked her in French if she desired a table. She shook her head and hastily walked on.

After the next connecting door, she stood still on the segmented, moving metal floor between the two cars. Draskovich was in the next one, and she wanted to pull herself together. The rhythmic noise of the track was loud here, the sensation of speed, of the harsh force that pulled them along. Pulled all of this, pigskin suitcases, syphons of soda water, little silver vases with three carnations each (where did they get them from?), men, women, children, ladies in velvet seats with their heads against the crocheted covers, the seed of lovers or husbands still in their bellies, wallets with threatening letters and bank drafts in inside pockets of men's jackets, a vision of a railroad accident, not a derailment but a piling of the entire train against a mountain wall, all and everything pressed together into one homogeneous ball, limbs, wombs, bottles, flowers – I must stop this nonsense.

She opened the next door and entered that carriage. It had only three compartments, a different sort of doors with heavy curtains. It was hushed in there, a still more aloof kind of luxury. Tolcheff had told her that Draskovich was in the middle compartment. She saw him already, his curtain wasn't drawn. He was wearing a smoking jacket and reading a white paperback book, while eating something from a little bag beside him. He looked different from what she remembered, and then again dreamlike overfamiliar. Beyond reach, and at the same time – what? – not important enough for them to have followed him all this way.

XX. Saifnitz-Pontebba

Anna waited until she saw Tolcheff appear in the connecting passage between the carriages; then she knocked. But she put so little conviction in it that Draskovich didn't hear her. She tried his door and found it was unlocked.

In that moment she became quite calm and went in, leaving the door ajar, and sat half-way across from him, one knee over the other, before he was aware of her entrance and looked up.

He put the book face down in his lap, began a little smile, and said, 'Well, what an unexpected – '

But he's not a stupid man, she thought. Because he stopped abruptly after only those four words and jumped up, letting his book drop to the floor. He knew she wouldn't have come in there alone. He took a step towards the door, to lock it or maybe to pull the emergency cord which was above it, but that instant Tolcheff came in, closed the door behind him with his left hand, and pointed the pistol in Draskovich's face.

'Sit down, Mr Undersecretary,' he said. Anna studied Tolcheff's expression, he looked self-possessed to her, although he was very pale. Her spirits rose, and she stood up, taking away Draskovich's suit jacket, which had hung on a hook next to his seat. She went to bolt the door, closed the curtains, and posted herself in the far corner.

Draskovich sat down with the little smile still on his face.

He put his hand out towards the candies, but Tolcheff, who didn't quite see what Draskovich meant to do, struck it away. Draskovich clicked his tongue. 'No need to be rude, young man,' he said.

Tolcheff placed himself across from him. 'Let's not chat,' he answered.

'What do you want?' Draskovich asked, no longer smiling.

'In a few minutes, at Pontebba, you're getting off with us.'

'A kidnapping! You must be thinking you're in America.'

Tolcheff pointed with his left hand to the luggage rack where Draskovich's overcoat, neatly folded, was lying. 'Give him his coat, Ann,' he asked her, 'we don't want him like that,' and he nodded towards the silk jacket. 'Please make sure there's nothing in the pockets.'

'I see,' Draskovich said. 'You've taken it upon yourself to introduce the mores of America here. A deathbed promise to your American father, no doubt. Or do I remember he was fished out of the Morskoi Canal one day? I think that's what our files have.'

Anna had searched the pockets of the coat and tossed it to Draskovich. 'Don't answer him,' she said to Tolcheff.

'We're getting out through the off door on the left, Ann, away from the platform. There's no one in the next compartment. You go ahead, he goes in the middle. All right?'

'Yes.'

The train was almost imperceptibly slowing down. The darkness outside was still total. Tolcheff looked at his watch by holding his left arm up in his line of vision on Draskovich. 'Seven fifty, Middle European time,' he said.

The train was braking strongly now. Lights ran over the faces of the two men sitting opposite each other at the window. Anna stood up and unlocked the door.

'Move,' Tolcheff said. 'Stand up.'

Draskovich crossed his legs and stared at him. His coat slid to the floor.

The train came to a stop, doors slammed. 'Pontebba!' someone cried outside.

'Stand up,' Tolcheff repeated, getting up himself.

Draskovich's little smile reappeared.

Tolcheff, who had not taken his eyes off him for an instant since entering the compartment, now glanced sideways at Anna.

'He won't do it!' Anna said.

'Pontebba, Pontebba,' from the voice outside.

'Shoot,' she cried. 'Shoot! Quick! Do it!'

Tolcheff did not react; he was as white as chalk.

'Oh damn you,' Anna screamed at him, 'you idiot – ' and she dived toward him to grab the pistol.

Tolcheff, almost automatically, moved his hand away from her.

She lost her balance. Tolcheff stepped back and bumped against the window: she kept on her feet by holding on to him, and closed her hand around his right wrist.

Someone knocked loudly on the door.

A frozen silence. Then Anna had the pistol, and held it under the left flap of her open coat, aimed at Draskovich.

In the doorway an Italian official appeared, in black uniform and plumed bersagliere hat. 'La dogana italiana, preparino il bagaglio, anything to declare, rien à déclarer?' he asked in a singsong voice, with a charming smile taking in all three of them.

She sat down beside Draskovich, the pistol through her coat pushed in his side.

XXI. Pontebba-Udine

If the customs man noticed anything unusual in the atmosphere of the compartment, he didn't show it. Perhaps he thought he had walked in on a jealous quarrel. 'Transit?' he asked, and when Tolcheff nodded, he just glanced in the various suitcases of Draskovich. But when he closed the door behind him, the train had started rolling again.

Anna shoved herself a foot or two away from Draskovich, so that he couldn't reach her in any sudden move. She made a gesture with her head towards the door, and Tolcheff got up and bolted it.

She bit her lip to fight off a spell of dizziness. She and Tolcheff had changed roles in a way, but she didn't feel any pleasure in that. What drained her was the realisation that she would have fired if she had had the time, that she would have tried to kill a man.

Tolcheff was looking at her as if waiting for more bitter reproaches. She moved herself still farther towards the door, to be able to have them both in view without moving her head. 'I'm sorry, Andrew,' she said. She didn't try to explain those unexpected words.

There was a silence, broken by Draskovich clearing his throat. They turned their eyes on him as if they saw him for the first time; he appeared unshaken by the whole business. Then Anna focused on his hands only. They're almost pudgy, she thought, and the nails are bitten. He was biting his nails in his office. He's not an abstraction, he is a person, he was given birth to, think of the long years for those fingers to be formed, and to grow, and to get in place and all that. . . . As for Tolcheff, Draskovich's black tie and silk jacket took him back to that reception where he had first seen him and heard his voice (a story about an ambassador caught with a boy). But personal dislike has nothing to do with this. It mustn't.

'Don't be ashamed, young man,' Draskovich said to him, 'because she's more determined than you. It's not really like that. With women these acts are personal, not political.'

Tolcheff jumped up, and Draskovich drew his head back sharply as if he was afraid he'd get a slap in the face. Tolcheff ignored him; he pulled Draskovich's suitcases down again, careful to stay out of Anna's line of vision, and began shaking out their contents on his seat.

'Help yourself,' Draskovich said. And went on, addressing

Anna now, 'I know you would shoot. But what Andy the Fix here doesn't know is, that it is not for your friend Sophia or for any Cause. It's personal spite. You see, Andy, she was my girl friend once. But I got tired of her very quickly.'

Tolcheff, searching through Draskovich's clothes, only said, 'Why don't you keep quiet.'

'You don't believe me. Shall I describe her to you? Small breasts, like tea saucers.' He drew a curve on the steamed-over window. 'A narrow middle. Ribs everywhere. Like sleeping with a schoolboy – Well, you see? Or haven't you been honoured yet with the lady's favours?'

'Oh, you know us anarchists,' Tolcheff answered without looking up. 'We share our women all around. I don't care.'

He glanced at Anna and gave her a kind of wink. Thank God, he's taken hold of himself.

'Look,' he said to her. 'Here's what I found. A Webley. All loaded.' He held up the dull black pistol.

'Ha, ha,' Draskovich said slowly. His face showed that he was about to make a biting comment, but as Tolcheff paid no attention, he muttered something inaudible and fell silent.

Tolcheff, pushing clothes and toiletries aside, sat down in the middle of the seat, crossing his legs, and leaned his hand with the pistol on his knee, the pistol trained on Draskovich.

'Why do you travel with the wardrobe of an English country gentleman, Draskovich?' he asked. 'That's not what you are, is it?'

'Don't get carried away with yourself, Andy the Fix, don't get smart,' Draskovich answered. 'Listen you two. Shooting me won't do you or Derkheim a bit of good. To the contrary. It'll create a mood in France – they'll immediately agree to extradition. On the other hand, I am prepared to make a deal.'

Tolcheff looked speculatively at him.

Draskovich's little smile was back. 'If you want to be efficient, don't risk your own usefulness, and your life, by attacking me. Concentrate on the system. You're an idealist, aren't you? I, on the other hand, am not. I don't give a damn

Anything reasonable, and I'm your man.'

'When is the next stop, Andrew?' Anna asked.

'Venice, at midnight.' He stood up and rang the service bell. 'Well,' he replied to Draskovich, 'you can begin by ordering dinner here in the compartment. For yourself and, eh, friends. I'm sure they'll be happy to oblige you.'

'Is that safe?' Anna asked him.

'It's safe,' Tolcheff said. 'There are no more bluffs to be called, and he knows it. I'm starved, aren't you?'

There was a sudden high spirits about him: she didn't understand why.

Draskovich looked from one to the other and started biting his thumbnail with a great concentration. 'Where did you two come from?' he asked. 'Did you follow me all this way?'

When they didn't react, he went on, more to himself it seemed, 'Incredible that they let you on in Petersburg . . . wait till I get hold of those fellows there.'

XXII. Udine-Pordenone (I)

Now the train had come down from the mountains, and was running through the plains of Venezia Giulia. The vast mist of the evening enveloped the landscape. Nothing was visible but an occasional farm light blinking unsteadily as if it were a star, and when the track curved, one or two green signal lights could be seen ahead, colouring the air. There was the rattle of iron bridges passed over, such short ones that the cadence was already cut off again after two or three girders – little streams running south, for the train had now entered the watershed of the Adriatic. The steam pipes in the carriages were still hissing, but it was a different kind of winter outside, no longer the grim one of eastern Europe. Here people were still out on the road, though invisible in the fog; peasants on their way to a café in Campoformio or Codroipo.

To them, the train flew by like an unreachable miracle, like a piece of a city street with its brightly lit shops and restaurants, a place they had been told about but never seen. Ladies in low dresses, with jewels, fox capes, men in black and white with faces showing that they owned the earth. Seats of dark red velvet, tables with softly shining electric lamps. They didn't see all of this, there was only time for an image here and there, a face in one car, a waiter filling a crystal wineglass near the window of another. It dissolved into a streak of light.

Every one of them who saw the train go by stood still, and looked after it until the red tail-lights had lost themselves in the hazy night.

None of them thought of himself as ever travelling like that, they could not possibly have felt envy. They were mostly silent, though, as they walked on. The train was not their enemy, but, in an obscure way, it showed them the invincibility of an inimical world.

XXIII. Udine-Pordenone (II)

All they had decided to order in the compartment were sandwiches. Draskovich had also asked for wine, which they let him drink by himself. 'They're beautiful sandwiches though, you must admit,' Anna said, picking the roast beef and smoked salmon out from between the bread and stuffing it in her mouth. She ate the bread by itself afterwards.

'You'll have your dining-car dinner one day. I promised

you,' Tolcheff told her.

Draskovich said, 'If you two don't mind. I'd like to settle this matter. What do you plan to do now?'

No answer.

'I'm not a policeman,' Draskovich went on. 'It's a role I play. A role I'm paid to play. I say what I'm expected to say, expected by my boss, the Minister of the Interior. And, mind you,' and he wagged his finger, 'expected by the people brought before me. You can have your Sophia Derkheim. I have no feelings in the matter, I am a businessman.'

'Maidenish into the grave,' Anna muttered.

He didn't quite catch her words and looked suspiciously at her.

'I know,' he started again. 'I may have given a different impression. That talk we had. I tell you, it – is – just – a – role.' He looked at his things strewn around. 'When you buy a suit, won't the salesman tell you how fine the material is, or how becoming? Even if he knows it isn't. When you meet him after hours, he won't insist. Well, this is after hours.'

He emptied his glass thirstily.

'What do you have to offer,' Tolcheff said.

'I'll give you my word of honour that I'll drop the extradition request.'

Anna, who had been poking with one foot in Drasko-vich's clothes (she had pushed them under the seat for the waiter), brought out a tweed jacket.

'Look, Andrew,' she said, 'why don't you change to a jacket and slacks of his? That outfit of yours mustn't see the light of another day. It's turning yellow.'

'His stuff won't fit me. He's fatter.'

'Oh, but do help yourself,' Draskovich said.

'You said that before,' she told him very offhandedly. 'What do you care? Maybe you won't need any clothes at all tomorrow. We'll fix it with pins,' she said to Tolcheff. 'When the waiter has been. Or better, I'll put up this.' She took the DO NOT DISTURB sign that had been hanging on the inside of the door, hung it outside, and bolted the door once more.

'It's not so easy, you know, to kill someone,' Draskovich informed her.

And she replied, not speaking to him but to Tolcheff, 'It is a weird business. That's what I was thinking about all this time. All you do is tense your finger, and a bullet penetrates the skin of another creature, a fantastic pain I expect, but you don't feel it, you just sit there, and the other is swung out into darkness, obliterated . . .'

Tolcheff reached out to Anna with his left hand, without looking at her, for he kept his eyes on Draskovich. He patted her and asked, 'What was that?'

'My knee.'

'Good.'

'What I wanted to point out,' Draskovich began, dabbing his face with his handkerchief. He was hot, even nervous perhaps.

'I shouldn't have screamed at you. It's courage, to think and to hesitate,' she answered Tolcheff.

'I'll tell you about it. Not now. It wasn't like that.'

'What I wanted to point out,' Draskovich said, 'is that you don't have to take my word for anything. Upon arrival in Cannes, we will all three proceed straight to the Central Post Office. I will there send one telegram to the president of the Marseilles court, formally withdrawing the extradition request. I will send another to Petersburg, saying that for reasons of state policy, the affair must be dropped. Only when you've seen me do that, you'll release me. And I won't try and countermand them later. Do you think I want to make a fool of myself, saying I was forced? Me, a head of police? I'll think up reasons. Relax. You have won.'

There was a silence.

'I can write those telegrams now,' he added, 'if you give me back my dispatch case.' He pointed to the heavy leather case which Tolcheff had put beside him, to lean his hand on with the Webley pistol.

'Won't you be met at the Cannes station, Mr

Draskovich?' Anna asked blandly.

He hesitated a fraction of a second before he answered, 'No, absolutely not. My trip has not been announced.'

'He's lying,' she said to Tolcheff.

'Yes, of course he is.'

'Well, you two think about it,' Draskovich said. 'I'm going to sleep. But please remember that shooting me will get you nowhere.'

He kicked off his shoes and stretched out on the seat. He covered himself with his coat, and turned away from them.

'Nor will kidnapping,' he then suddenly added, speaking with his face to the back of the seat. 'My government is much more interested in principles than in me. If he has to sacrifice me, the Minister will sigh, and then he'll go right ahead and do it. In fact, he'll enjoy thinking of the entry for his memoirs, a lot of fancy stuff about the terrible conflict between duty and personal feeling. Good night.'

XXIV. Pordenone-Conegliano (I)

Draskovich was asleep, or pretending to be. They didn't care.

'Are you tired?' he asked her.

'No – You?'

'No.'

'It's still misty out.'

'Yes.'

The train was very quiet, no doors, no voices; only the perfectly regular rhythm of the rail ties, coming very close together, as if they were going even faster than before.

'We must talk,' Anna said, 'to make sure we don't fall asleep. And to reach a decision.'

'Venice is the next stop. But Venice is bad. It's a dead end, and it's a head station with one exit. It's a night-life place, things are still hopping there at midnight. There'll be too many people.'

'You're still in favour of the hostage plan then?' she asked.

'Well, yes . . . I don't believe they'd sacrifice an under-secretary for Sophia. It's not even that, they wouldn't want to admit he was a prisoner. They couldn't afford such a show of weakness right on top of Sophia's trial. I think they'd just drop the case.'

'Maybe.'

'It's a good chance.'

'Where would we try then?'

He took his notebook out of his pocket with his left hand and held it out to her.

'Milan. It's the first important stop after Venice, with something like a ten-minute wait. And it'll be in the dead of night. Four a.m., I think. You look.'

She leafed through the notebook. 'Here. Four fifteen. Friends in Milan?'

He laughed a bit self-consciously. 'No.'

'That boarding-house, with the deserters?'

'It'd be a long way back. Perhaps we should look the other way now, west. . . . Yes, actually Genoa would perhaps be better still. Easier to get away from.'

'If we can keep him under control like this, once it gets light, with waiters and attendants bustling about. Will it be light in Genoa?' she asked.

'Just about. Genoa would be just right, I guess.'

When she didn't say anything more, he came out with, 'Ann, I've botched up everything quite terribly so far. Right?'

I'm not going to hold his hand for him. She shook her head. 'Tell me about Bakunin.'

'Now?'

'It will keep us awake.'

'Don't count on it,' he said. She's suggesting that as if I were one of the children in her school, to stop me from

73

whining. Damnation. I better pull myself together.

'Did you ever see a portrait of him?' he asked. 'A big man, but pathetic sort of, vulnerable, I think. Full of wild ideas, bad ones too, I guess. But such a – I don't know, such guts. He spent something like ten years in a Prussian jail, in chains, for nothing really. It didn't unnerve him. Love for the people. Belief that the people are good. The very opposite, the very precise antithesis of men like him.' He pointed at Draskovich with his foot.

'Do you love the people?'

'Yes.'

'You were known at home as a rather nasty fellow. Rude, too.'

'Don't be trivial, Ann,' he said sternly. 'I love the people; I don't love people.'

'I beg your pardon. Don't the two go together?'

'But no! Every petty dictator, every damn king and president loves people, pats dogs, accepts flowers from little girls. That has no political meaning. Justice! If you want friendliness, we should stick to feudalism. There was surely a lot of love and friendliness in that, you know. . . . Now we have the war of all against all.'

'Tell me something about how you grew up.'

Tolcheff disliked thinking of his own youth. Questions about it he always answered, as he did now, 'I'm the New Man. I started full-grown, like Minerva.'

After a while he asked, 'Why did you really come on this expedition?'

'For Sophia.'

'But there's more to it?'

'He offended – ' She paused. 'He offended the dignity of my womanhood. I don't mean to sound pompous.'

'You don't. But is that all?'

'All?'

'I mean, you told me yesterday that you were through with quote all that unquote. "All that" being Bakunin, justice, the whole business.'

'I am,' she said. 'I am no longer interested. Precisely

74

because I, at my age, and different from your Bakunin, don't believe people are good. No longer believe people are good. In fact, screw them all. You can all gobble each other up, I don't care.'

'But I don't understand how you can make that kind of statement. Think of it, we've just started a new century. "A new time is beginning."'

She shrugged impatiently. 'I'm sure history or nature don't give a damn if the year has two noughts or not. That's just our bookkeeping.'

'And your teaching? And the youth council?'

'Oh! That's something else, Tolcheff. I believe in children. I believe in innocence. I believe in protecting a child's innocence with everything I've got, with a pistol, with my nails. Children enter this world, we bring them into it, and they look around with surprised eyes, waiting to see what it is like, waiting for warmth, softness, just protection really. And milk. Nothing more than a cat gives its young, or a monkey. How disgusting we are, we don't even manage that.'

An image of Sophia of her standing alone at the school gate, it must have been the first term, we were both ten or eleven. She was so gangly and awkward, she looked younger. Why had she been crying? I don't remember what had happened, just that image of a summer afternoon, heavy foliage, the smell of sun on leaves, girls happily running off home or earnestly talking together.

Sophia with her tear-streaked face, hot looking; the sun was shining on her stringy hair. I think it was the first time I was conscious of someone being ugly. And just that second I felt that life, all of life, was maybe not the great beckoning adventure I thought it was, but a great sadness.

Anna thought that perhaps that moment had prevented her from ever becoming good friends with Sophia.

But it binds us, in a different way.

XXV. Pordenone-Conegliano (II)

Draskovich, under his coat, looked at the buttoned velvet of the seat in front of his face. He heard the voices of Tolcheff and Anna but he didn't try to listen. He fixed his attention on the velvet and ducked deeper under the coat.

Immediately he felt he had to answer this question for himself: was it a lie or the truth that he wasn't a policeman, that it was all an act? I like to think that. I like to see myself, playing a role. But then why am I trying to lure them into that Cannes telegram deal? But damn it, it is surely natural that I don't want to be duped. Self-preservation.

But suppose the Minister said, 'I leave it to you, I don't care.' I'd still want that Derkheim girl extradited, punished, and dead. Why? That Judge she tried to shoot, he's an old swine, he deserves twenty years himself for all the tricks he's pulled – he thinks we don't know, he's stupid on top of everything else. What then? Because people like the Derkheims try to make a virtue out of being left out? And because the Judge's tricks are our kind of tricks, don't threaten us? Us, our? Who are 'our'? I don't believe in any we's and our's.

How could I? There's nothing outside my skin. I want sun on it, I hate cold, I like it to be touched by good silk shirts, and by women. I can't step outside it. God, the Romans had parties, in that book about Petronius, or by Petronius?, slaves covered in pitch were burned alive by way of illumination – chained to posts around the terraces. Their tongues out, I'd assume. There you stand with your glass of wine. Did they have glass then? I admit I would have wanted to see that. What more proof do you need that

I am I and he is he, and there's no bridge and no link? But Derkheim and her Judge. I missed the point there. The point is, of course, that there's a link between Derkheim's fate and the silk on my skin, while there's no such link with the Judge's dirty tricks. Power, nothing us or ours. I am I. Too simple? Maybe.

I'm not going to go in for any heroics though. Precisely because of that. No jumping or wrestling or running. I knew in Pontebba he would not shoot. Now he will.

That fellow we were holding, the day before I left. Incredible, that he let himself die instead of helping us. Die, vanish, disappear. He couldn't even think, I'm leaving a better world behind, or my friends this or that. When you're dead, there is no I and no world and no My friends. Then why did he? Pride, hatred of me maybe.

I'm curious why Andy the Fix is now quite ready to take a shot at me. It must be her doing. A scientific deduction: no other factor has changed. She gives him the strength. If I'd get them separated . . . I wonder if that would do it, if on his own he'd be the old Andy the Fix again who can't hurt a fly. I'd know looking at him. I knew that report was crap, about him being an agent or an organiser. You can tell he isn't, just by looking at his hands, like a woman's hands.

It must be all her doing then. But, of course. How stupid of me, to think he had sent her to me. Damn. Why didn't I understand it was all her idea? To save her friend Sophia. Or because of that dead brother, Michael Derkheim. Those two were screwing each other, I bet you. I'm here through my own sloppiness. There are always links. When you get one, you must bring in the whole bunch, girl friends, boy friends, maybe-boy friends, grandfathers – there's always a link.

He felt a drop of sweat roll along his forehead. Oh, stop it, he told himself. What is the matter with me. Those are thoughts for behind my desk. Stop it. I'm not behind my desk. I'm trying to sleep in my clothes, with two people holding pistols at me.

I should join them.

He got quite excited about that idea. Stay in France, ask

77

for asylum, I've always secretly helped the other side. Revelations by a Former Head of Police. Interviews, admiration suddenly from all those fucking journalists, girl students crawling in your bed – it would be amusing.

He laughed soundlessly. I must kick that possibility around for a bit.

Perhaps it isn't so promising after all. They'd never believe me. Or if they did, I'd have become useless to them. A defecting undersecretary cannot do a thing for them. Petersburg would let our Third Section man in the Paris Embassy handle the extradition, that idiot, what's his name, Zidkin, with his striped socks and those nature-lover shoes with all the leather pieces. He better stay out of my way, Zidkin. I can just see him ruin my Cannes vacation, with that nasal penetrating French of his he thinks so wonderful –

For now he had dismissed the situation he was in, and he started visualising the things he'd do in Cannes. The good smell of the air, those pine trees; you felt more potent the moment you got off the train. That girl who always stands on the corner of the Croisette and the, the Rue Pasteur after six, a blow job for just ten francs, if you give me twenty, I'll do it very very slowly, très lentement, chéri.

He fell asleep.

XXVI. Conegliano-Venice

Tolcheff was sitting up alone. He liked that. Doing guard duty. He listened to the peaceful breathing of Anna, curled up in her corner, and to the unpleasant noises Draskovich was making. He must be sleeping, too, he wouldn't produce those on purpose. He is too vain for that.

Vanity. Perhaps that was the handle to the man. Tell him

that defecting, coming over to our side, would make him a public figure. I've always thought of him as cruel and lazy. That isn't quite right. His cruelty is of a particular kind; he's never supposed to be present at interrogations when things get brutal. He is lazy. He himself would probably call it hedonistic or something. It's important to understand him, in order to get the better of him.

Trying to kill him is useless, he is right about that. I could do it, though, if I had to.

Tolcheff had never fired a pistol before, but friends had shown him how to load and clean one and how you could tell if there was a cartridge in the chamber. I've seen this model before, it's the new Webley; but taking it apart and oiling it on a kitchen table is very different from holding it like this, my fist around its handle, its barrel pointed at another man. I like the feel of its weight. It's comfortable, pleasant even. It makes me unweary. The cool weight of a weapon in your hand.

Oh, watch it, Tolcheff. Stop right there. Cool weight my ass. Don't let this turn me into a know-nothing Hungarian dragoon after all. It is an obscene business, to attack someone else's body. I know what Ann means, but there is more to it even. To tear a hole in that body . . . obscene is precisely the word. Worse perhaps than cannibalism. You're not to forget that, even if you have a little machine that does it for you.

He decided to go over Draskovich's possessions. A clue to his character.

First he put the tweed jacket beside him on the seat, then he fished out a pair of slacks from the other clothes and put that with it. He did all this with his left hand; his right hand stayed in place.

A box of jewellery, hard to open with one hand. He took out two gilded or gold safety pins, he'd use those to keep Draskovich's pants up. Shoes, no less than four pairs. But they were round and short; he'd have to stick to his Warsaw patent-leather pair.

White shirts, but without collars. There was a round box

of collars and cuffs. Too complicated. A yellow sports shirt, very soft, silk maybe. That would do fine. Toiletries. He took out a razor, a brush, and a little round soap dish. He needed those. Then there were more jackets, trousers, a linen suit, dozens of socks and handkerchiefs, cummerbunds in red and black, nightshirts.

A hatbox: a claque top hat, a panama, a linen yacht cap. A leather case with little bottles, a purple powder for the teeth, 'Birkenwasser' (a picture on the bottle showed a Byronic gentleman wetting his curls with it), and a black substance in a flacon with brushes strapped on – did Draskovich dye his hair? Something called Agua de Vetiver, pastilles and powders in little boxes with French labels in fine print on them. Crystal, silver bottle caps, leather. He surely needs a lot of things to keep going.

Novels. Andrea Nerciat, De Latouce – funny blank covers – but it's all pornographers! Old ones at that. I've seen this one, we passed it around in high school. I remember, the hero had a disease I didn't understand and he was washing his prick in mercury and sulphur, our copy had an etching showing him at it. It just made you itchy. I wonder what Draskovich finds in these.

A vague memory made him feel dirty; he shifted closer to the window and pulled at the brass handle at the top. To his surprise it slid down smoothly. In our trains you have to be a prize fighter to open a window. He pulled it down about three inches, and pushed the books out one by one. Ne pas se pencher en dehors. É pericoloso sporgersi. Why not in Russian, don't they mind if we break our necks? He was about to close the window again, but then he took his notebook out of his pocket, wriggled out of his dinner jacket, dress shirt, and black trousers, and pushed the lot out after the novels. Standing in his underwear and black shoes, the Webley in one hand, he felt there was something very cheerful and satisfactory in what he was doing. He now threw out the pastilles, the hair dye, the tooth powder, then the socks and the handkerchiefs. The cummerbunds. He lowered the window another inch and out went the jewellery box. Then all the clothes except the things he meant to wear. He tried to throw them wide, he didn't want them to be run over by the train. They should be found and used.

He carefully closed the window and the blind. A secret policeman sows his clothes all along an Italian railroad line. It must be at least a mile long, the Draskovich presentation. He imagined the peasants of Venezia province, one wearing a Paris nightshirt, another a hat from Willoughby after dyeing his hair black from those little bottles. All those articles which once must have been the subject of long deliberation in stores, correspondence on ministerial paper with London and Paris tailors. He closed the empty suitcases and put them back on the rack. Then he put on the shirt, the trousers, and the jacket.

All this took a very long time, for he moved softly and kept one hand and one eye on Draskovich, just in case he'd suddenly jump up. He sat down, realised he hadn't come upon any papers yet, and opened the dispatch case in his lap.

In doing that, there was a kind of indecency. Going beyond a line. Once someone's life is under threat, there is no limit. Like a conquered country, anything can be demanded as long as there's hope of survival left. That time when I was arrested in Moscow, I knew it was a mistake, but the shock was – the shock was the ease with which the policeman opened my wallet, looked at my letters and photos. It seemed so shameless. As if I had stopped to matter, stopped to be, almost. It goes in stages. The final one is when they're going to kill you, then nothing matters, nothing makes a difference any more, I mean if you held on to a door, they might as well cut off your hand.

He opened the case nonetheless. It had a compartment with a flacon of ink and two little gold pens – more leather and silver – writing pads, some with the letterhead of the Ministry. A folded document with a seal, accrediting Draskovich as an emissary of the Ministry of the Interior. A diplomatic laissez-passer: 'Lectori Salutem. May all courtesy and assistance . . .' Two chequebooks on the Crédit Lyonnais, one in the name of Draskovich, one with a number and letters, some kind of government account no doubt. No money. A notebook with names and addresses, a hodgepodge of towns, barbers, tailors, massage salons, women's first names, and just people. He put it all back.

He closed the case, and propped it up once more under his right arm.

XXVII. Venice

The train had been racing south through the dark unmarked plain. The fog had withdrawn into rolls tucked away in hollows of the fields. The air was clear and so full of stars that Tolcheff, lifting an edge of the blind, could see them even with the light on in the compartment.

Of a sudden the engine left the land and plunged on to the causeway across a lagoon. Now the train was encased between the sky and the black water reflecting rows of lights all along the horizon, as if in a shell of two skies touching.

Then, equally abruptly, it was inside the station of Venice, under its high glass dome. White electric light, a whir of activities, passengers, porters, shouts, voices, even music from somewhere.

Anna sighed and went on sleeping. Draskovich woke up and immediately sat upright. He swallowed and stared at Tolcheff. 'I'm thirsty,' he said. 'Allow me to treat you to a coffee.' He raised the blind and opened the window without waiting for an answer, and hailed one of the vendors going up and down the platform.

The coffees were served in little cups on a tray with glasses of water; a boy waited at their window to redeem them. Draskovich took his cigarette case out of the pocket of his silk jacket and produced a three-rouble note from it for the boy. He waved away the change. 'Never carry change in your pockets,' he told Tolcheff. 'It spoils the line of your clothes.'

'I'll remember that.'

Draskovich put the case beside him on the seat and tried to brush the wrinkles out of his jacket.

'You don't seem to carry much money,' Tolcheff remarked, closing the window and the blind.

'You must have seen my chequebooks. Don't apologise, I'd have looked, too. I prefer cheques on all occasions. It is very disadvantageous to change roubles all the time. Take my advice.'

Tolcheff smiled.

'You don't have many roubles,' Draskovich half asked, half stated. 'Never mind, you don't know how much those change bureaus steal. Here, give me those chequebooks for a moment.'

He filled in a cheque with one of the pens, tore it out, and tossed it at Tolcheff. Then he threw both chequebooks back into the dispatch case which Tolcheff had kept open on his knee. The cheque fluttered to the floor.

'Don't shoot me,' Draskovich said as he bent over to pick it up. 'Here.'

Tolcheff looked down in his lap. Five thousand francs.

'At any branch of the Crédit Lyonnais,' Draskovich announced. 'You'll find one within walking distance of your hotel, wherever it is.'

Tolcheff didn't answer.

'In Cannes, I personally always stay in the Hôtel du Parc,' Draskovich chatted on. 'It's excellent, and for some reason you don't stumble over those rich Russian tourists there. After all, you don't need to go to France to see them. I can heartily recommend it.'

He sighed. 'You think this is all part of some trick of mine. You overestimate me, I told you it's after hours. That cheque is on a government account, money that belongs as much to you as to me, in a manner of speaking.'

'Not a very subtle move on your part, though,' Tolcheff

said, picking up the cheque with his left hand and studying it.

'It's not a bribe. Tear it up if you want. It's just a token of my good faith. You see, I know you're in on this only because of her.' He pointed with his head towards Anna. 'That's fine with me. Men do all sorts of things to catch a woman's attention. But let's talk man to man. By some freak of circumstance you've got a certain momentary power over me. It isn't much. The moment you use it, it will be gone for ever, used up. For what? That is up to you. To kill me? We've already gone over that. For Miss Derkheim? Do you really give a damn? All right, you don't want her sent back to Russia. I'll offer you that, and more. I'll give you La Derkheim. To let you keep face with her' (another nod towards Anna's corner) 'and her crowd. That may be useful. See how easy? I give her to you. And why not? That Judge she shot was an old swine. For instance, the house he bought for himself this last summer, "Mon Repos" or something, he stole bodily out of that harbour dues lawsuit.'

In an oddly raw voice he interjected, ' "Mon Repos"! The fucking nerve!' and went on, 'Then I suggest that you come over to our side of the fence.'

'To be a police spy?'

'God, no,' Draskovich said impatiently. 'I don't employ amateurs. I'm offering you and me a painless way out of this embarrassment. You don't know what to do with me any more. I don't want the risk of a bullet in some painful place when Miss Anna loses her nerve. Do you know why I'm giving you that cheque? Because you don't even know what life is all about. I'd like you to know.'

'That's very generous.'

'You're surprised, aren't you? You didn't know people like me had complicated feelings, did you? This train, tomorrow afternoon, will arrive in Cannes, right?'

He seemed to wait for an answer.

'Right,' Tolcheff said warily.

'Let's assume we'll all still be on it. All right. You step out of the station, you walk down the street to the Esplanade. It's only a few blocks. But what blocks! Smart bars, shops for women, but smart, nothing like Nevski Prospect, you see. Jewellers. What do I say, jewellers. Grocers! Grocers with hams and sausages and partridges made to look like jewels! Women. Those few blocks of a French town are more sensual than a whole street of brothels in Russia or in Germany. Sensual. You reach the Esplanade. The sun is low, shining over the sea, you can't believe your eyes. The air is quiet, all you hear is voices and the wheels of carriages over the boulevard, a smooth macadamised boulevard, mind you, no Russian potholes. You see women. Not persons of the female gender, but women as the crown of creation, with their clothes, and their colours, and their perfumes, everything, pointing one way – desire. Imagine how you'll think back to that when you're old! Imagine how sorry you will be if you missed out! Now do you understand? You want to miss out on all that for your cold-water affairs in a Petersburg attic, for those thin girls who talk and talk and talk when what a man wants is a soft body under him?'

A whistle sounded through his last words, and the train started to back out of the station.

'You see, Andrew,' Draskovich said, 'you don't know anything. We're not interested in beating up students. Men need power because they need money. Men need money because they have senses. That is reality. You people don't know. You make speeches about hungry peasants. We're not peasants. You're a sensitive man, I can tell from your hands. You don't know what sensations there are in store for you in this world. But it takes money.'

Tolcheff, without speaking, put the cheque in the left pocket of the tweed jacket.

'Zidkin,' Draskovich said. 'That's our man in France. When that money is gone, see him for more. For a new passport. For good counsel. Anything. Zidkin with the shoes. Zidkin.'

XXVIII. Venice-Padua

Then Draskovich announced, 'Excuse me, but I have to piss.'

Several times Tolcheff had heard steps outside, of people going by. 'I can't risk it,' he said.

'You must be joking. After all we said?'

'You can use the washbasin. Anna's asleep.'

'No, I cannot. I'm not a damn student.'

Tolcheff pulled the window all the way down. The stars had become obscured, and out of a uniform darkness a wet but not very cold wind blew in his face. 'Piss out of the window.'

'After all we said,' Draskovich muttered, positioning himself in the corner and standing on his toes to reach over.

'We didn't say anything. You said a lot, and I listened.'

'Hello,' loudly from Anna. 'How are you, Andrew? How is the prisoner? Are you airing this place? It feels good. I'm going to wash my face, and then I'll take over from you.'

'I'm wide awake,' Tolcheff told her. 'But I'd like to change places for a while, I'm tired of staring at him.'

Draskovich sat back in his corner, with his coat draped over his shoulders. He seemed to gaze through the window, which he had closed with a shiver, but the reflection showed his furious face.

He finally turned his head to Anna, who had come back to sit across from him, a foot or so away from the wall, her feet tucked under her and with the pistol in her lap.

'You may as well know,' he told her, 'I made your friend an offer, but I think now that I wasted my time. I don't know why you brought him along. You and I may feel different about things, but at least we know where we stand.

We're both professionals. That's what counts.'

'Yes,' Anna said. 'True.'

'He gave me five thousand francs,' Tolcheff told her.

'He did? What for?'

'Like hell he did,' Draskovich broke in. 'You just try cashing that cheque without delivering.'

'Delivering?' Anna asked.

'Oh, let's stop repeating words like children,' Draskovich said to her, half turning his back on Tolcheff. 'I tried to explain some facts of life to him. You see, he can't win, and I can't lose.'

'I see, Mr Undersecretary.'

'Maybe I'm through with that undersecretary stuff. Look at it this way. Your friend Tolcheff can go on the way he is now, scrounging around, discussing causes with girls like you – or he can join us. Yes, that's what I offered him. But you see, it makes no real difference. Either way, he's nobody, so who cares? That's what I meant with, he can't win. Now I, I can't lose. You'll ask why. Because if I turn it around, if I don't ask you to join me, but if I join you – if I defect, ask asylum in France, I'll still be somebody. You see? If I announce I'll start behaving like Tolcheff here already does every day, there'll be articles in the papers, interviews, pictures, it'll be news. And it's your people, your friends, who'll be doing the interviewing and the writing of the articles.'

'You got me confused,' Anna said.

'It's simple enough. There's only one set of values in this world. Power which is money which is power. The underground, the Reds, the anarchists, the revolutionaries, the liberals, whatever you call yourselves, can't get away from it, don't you see? They'll all come running to meet a defected undersecretary. They don't give a monkey's fuck about a shabby journalist who's been all theirs, all his life.'

'A monkey's fuck,' Anna repeated thoughtfully.

'So it's all the same to me,' Draskovich said. 'You can join me, or I can join you. Either way, we break this dead-lock.'

'But suppose we don't want you to join us?' from Tolcheff

'I knew you wouldn't understand what I've just told you It's not up to you, Andy my boy. I know who to see ir France. When I tell him I've come to save Derkheim, do you think he'll ask your opinion first?'

'So it's really six of one and half a dozen of the other? Anna asked.

'Precisely.'

'Well, why don't we toss a coin,' she suggested cheerfully. 'Heads, we'll all be revolutionaries; tails, we'll be cops and informers.'

'We can't do that,' Tolcheff said. 'And you know why. We don't keep change in our pockets. It spoils the line of our clothes.'

Draskovich stared at him. Tolcheff thought he was going to spit on the floor in his direction, but he didn't. 'I think I'll try to go back to sleep,' he said. 'Call me if you've anything real to say.'

'By the way, Mr Draskovich,' Tolcheff asked, 'how were you going to pay for all your expenses on this train if you only carry a few roubles?'

Draskovich did not answer.

'By cheque, I guess,' Tolcheff went on. 'They'd know who you are, of course. But suppose we took you up on that idea of those telegrams in Cannes, how would you pay for them? We haven't got a penny.'

'The French postal services accept my cheque, too,' Draskovich said.

'Oh. But what about the waiter then? And the carriage attendant? You can't tip them with cheques, can you?'

Draskovich shrugged impatiently. 'I keep a few notes for contingencies.'

'In a wallet?'

'In my cigarette case. Why? Are you a thief of money as well as clothes?'

'Hey, you don't mind my wearing this, do you? You'll get them back. Just a loan among future colleagues.'

Draskovich lay down on his seat, lit a cigarette, and blew out smoke rings towards the ceiling.

Tolcheff went to sit next to Anna and started a whispered conversation with her.

XXIX. Padua-Vicenza

Tolcheff touched Draskovich's shoulder. 'Before you sink into the sleep of the just – '

'Hmm?'

'We've decided to take you up on those telegrams. If you write them now.' He handed him the writing pad with the government letterhead and stood beside him.

'Are you going to dictate?' Draskovich asked angrily.

'No, no, go ahead. I'm just reading along to see what you make of it.'

'The President, Assizes Court, Marseilles A.M.,' Draskovich wrote. 'That means "Alpes-Maritimes,"' he told Tolcheff. 'On behalf of my government and superseding previous communications, I am withdrawing and cancelling all extradition requests in the case of Russian nationality convict Sophia Derkheim. We abide by the decision of French justice. Signed, Draskovich, Undersecretary in the Ministry of the Interior, Saint Petersburg.'

'Not what's called telegram style,' Tolcheff said.

'Well, you don't have to pay for it. But take out what you want.' He tore off the page and handed it to him.

'Next,' he said. 'His Excellency the Minister of the Interior, Fontanka, Saint Petersburg.

'Sir, with due respect and having taken full cognizance of local sensitivities and ramifications, I advise no further action in the criminal case of convict Sophia Derkheim. Signed, respectfully F R Draskovich, Undersecretary.'

He gave the pad and pen back. 'Satisfactory?'

'Yes.'

He lay down and lit a fresh cigarette. Tolcheff went back to his place beside Anna, and wrote on the next page:

'Counsellor Zidkin Imperial Russian Embassy Paris

'Interrupting journey for personal reasons stop arriving Cannes on express Wednesday December 26 instead of December 19 stop meet me then. Signed Draskovich.'

Then he wrote the same telegram addressed to 'Counsellor Zidkin, care of Hôtel du Parc, Cannes, A.M.'

'Why December 19, and 26?' Anna asked in an undertone.

'That's the date. It's the 18th now. No, the 19th already. The Gregorian calendar, remember? They're thirteen days ahead of Russia out here.'

He became aware of Draskovich looking at him from under half-closed eyelids.

'Just copying your telegrams, Drasky. For the record.'

He started another one. 'His Excellency the Minister of Foreign Affairs Quai d'Orsay Paris.

'Undersigned F R Draskovich police official Russian service arriving in France December . . . has resigned his function and requests asylum in the French Republic.'

He changed 'has resigned' to 'is resigning'. 'I'm just fiddling,' he said softly to Anna, 'trying it out.'

'Why are you two satisfied with those wires suddenly?' Draskovich asked, without stirring or taking his cigarette out of his mouth for more than a moment.

'Well – perhaps I've grown fond of my cheque,' Tolcheff said. 'I think I'd like to cash it.'

'Mr Undersecretary,' Anna said. She waited, until Draskovich finally turned his head towards her.

'Yes?'

'My father was in the Foreign Service. I remember him telling me that when you send service telegrams, there's a code or a number you use, to authenticate them.'

A silence.

Anna jumped up. 'See!' she cried, 'I told you not to listen to him! Now do you see! You and your damn cheque! Let's stop this nonsense, let's get this man out at Milan and if he drags his feet, let's shoot him and to hell with it. You're an idiot, Andrew Tolcheff!'

Draskovich raised himself. 'I mean to add the code number when we're standing at the telegraph window in the Cannes post office,' he said. 'You must see that makes sense, Tolcheff. I need some guarantee, too.'

'Cannes in a pig's eye,' Anna near screeched. 'In a monkey's fuck. Do you think we want to meet your buddies at the Cannes station and get ourselves arrested? Those telegrams go off in Milan, or never.'

'In Milan?'

'Yes, yes. And you're going to pay for them. With your cigarette case money.'

'There's an all-night post office in the Milan station,' Tolcheff told him.

Draskovich looked thoughtfully at her. 'Very well. If you insist. You must put "3S" after my name. That stands for "Third Section".'

'Which no longer exists,' Tolcheff said.

Draskovich stretched himself out again. 'We're a tradition-bound group.' He turned his head away from them.

Tolcheff wrote '3S' under his telegrams. 'I think you scared the truth out of him,' he whispered to her. 'But if he's still lying, we won't worry about it. Those codes never work so well. They'd probably say, "The telegram service in Italy is a mess." Are you sure you want to do it?'

'It's easier for a woman, they'll help me quicker. I'll take his briefcase, and say I'm his secretary if there's any question about them. Are you sure that office is open?'

'I've asked the conductor twice. It's on platform one. We come in on platform three. If you miss the train – '

'I won't. I'll time myself. I'm a teacher, remember, I'm very systematic. Just the two telegrams to Zidkin. What about the one in which he's defecting?'

'I figured if he isn't on this train, they'd believe it. But that would be the end then, we could never send any of the others afterwards.'

'Right. Let's try the two Zidkıns first. And after Milan make our final decision.'

'Our final final decision.'

Aloud she added, 'I still say it's a mistake. We'll do it your way, Andrew, but just this once more.'

Draskovich, however, was making his sleep noises again.

XXX. Vicenza-Montebello

They agreed they'd have a moratorium until Milan. Till then no more talking about Draskovich.

'Wouldn't it be nice, though,' she said, 'if we could really forget him. Say, shoot him full of morphine.'

'So much for the moratorium.'

'Shoot him period. In a tunnel when there's a lot of noise. And dump him in a river. You take him by the neck, and I take his feet.' She showed how they would together shove Draskovich out of the window.

He nodded. 'It's the logical thing to do. Iron logic, I guess. Throw him out when we cross the Po. Then wait a day and send the wires to the Marseilles court and to the Minister in Petersburg. Wait a few more days, and send the I've-defected message.

She thought about that. 'It would be without flaws.'

'It would, wouldn't it? They'd be suspicious in Petersburg, admitted, and they'd have an investigation. But if it were all published, if we sent copies to the big French newspapers, I don't see how they could ever start on Sophia again.'

'Right . . .' she said.

'Of course, we'd have to remove all identification. Bash up his face, maybe.'

They were getting more and more sombre. 'Oh damn,' he said, 'you know we won't do it. Not because we're too scared to, or too noble. Not because he isn't a murderer and a torturer and you name it, directly or by proxy.'

'It's against the principles of socialism.'

'Don't be ironic, Ann. It is.'

'I know why I don't. If I could open a trap door under his seat right now by pressing a button, I would. But I can't . . .' She made a grimace. 'It's not principles with me, it's just cowardice. Or if you want to be nice, call it disgust.'

'We'll handle it another way,' he said.

'What time is it now?'

'Almost one. Let's raise the blind and open the window a crack. He's beginning to smell. Or maybe it's us.'

The train had climbed out of the plains and was running under a clear sky once more. The moon had risen and was shining on the Venetian Alps at their right. The snow reflected its rays; it was as if a wavering radiance were floating in the distance. 'Oh, let's turn off the light, just for one minute,' Anna asked. 'I want to see. If he stirs, I'll conk him over the head with the pistol.'

When the compartment was dark except for the little night lamp, the mountains showed so sharply that even the pine trees and the valleys in the shade stood out. The light was so strong that it threw a shadow on the floor of the carriage. 'How pure the air must be,' Anna said. She was whispering. 'Is Italy very beautiful?'

'Yes.'

The expression on her face seemed so painfully longing in that light that it hurt him. From being defensive, he now felt the need to protect her: it hurt him to see her without her self-assurance. She has to be consoled like a child missing out on a treat. 'It's at its most beautiful when you're rushing through,' he said. 'It's a very poor country.'

'Oh, Andrew. Just look at those mountains. Just be a traveller for once.'

'But I am. I told you that, because I thought . . . Well, damn, it is poor. Desperately poor. Did you ever hear of a man called Malatesta? Maybe they'll surprise the world, maybe this will be the first country to go socialist.'

She pressed his hand.

'Does that mean, "please shut up"?'

'It means, you're a sweet man.'

'Sweet. God, I don't want to be sweet.'

'It is not a bad thing to be,' she said firmly. 'You know, I've been wondering why Draskovich's suitcases rattle so strangely in the rack. I hadn't noticed that before.'

'They're empty. I threw all his stuff out of the window.'

'What?' She began to giggle. 'Why?'

'I don't know really. It suddenly seemed a good thing to do.'

She tapped him on his cheek.

'Ann, I wonder – ' he began. But the moment had passed and he no longer felt the stronger of the two. He said, 'We better put the light on again.'

'One minute more. I want to remember this. I have to memorise it.'

XXXI. Montebello-Verona

Then, with their eyes adjusted, there was no reason to turn the overhead lamp back on. The moonlight covered the countryside with a soft white glow, and against the black air the mountains stood in a totality of white, dazzlingly sharp.

Confused thoughts whirled through Tolcheff's head. He remembered a remark she had made, perhaps only half joking, that he had planned this journey to have a fling with her; and the blood ran to his head. How stupid I've been. If I'd handled this expedition better, she'd have admired that, she would have had a new idea about what we're after, about how we try to be different people. It all started with the starter pistol. No, of course, it started at the border. My unforgivable mistake about the gauge. There is no excuse for a thing like that.

And then showing up after Warsaw in that lugubrious dinner jacket. Perhaps she had thought that funny, though. But did I have some farfetched motive? Surely I wasn't after her, but didn't I mean to impress her, because she always acted so, so unimpressible?

I'm still thinking along such lines. What's become of my self-discipline? Just do the job, damn it, for its own sake. What else for. But there's nothing wrong in hoping to convert her, to get her out of that icy cynicism, hopelessness really when you come to think of it. What did she say, screw you all, screw them all.

I'll get the chance, I'll create it.

And she will let me make love to her again. That couldn't have been a whim. She is much too virginal for that, too pristine almost; it must have had some meaning. But I was so terribly bad. Hell, damn, why do I make love to that damn Wenda like some kind of sex athlete, and with Ann I acted like a high school kid? It's unfair –

Ann's flat belly, her middle you could span with two hands, those cool eyes that looked so questioningly, when I made love to her. He took a deep breath, it sounded like a sigh.

But Anna was lost in looking at the mountains, and Tolcheff did not appear in her thoughts. She had never seen mountains before. I realise it's just a geological whatever, they're not closer to the sky and the stars than we are. All the same, what an amazing thing. How lovely it must be on those slopes, soundless, bathing in that light, motionless. The Swiss have a mountain called the Virgin. No man should be allowed to touch it. A baptism with snow. Of course we are born without sin.

'And what were you thinking of?' she asked him.

'Nothing really.'

She jumped up. She first pulled down the blind, and after

that switched the light back on. 'I didn't want to see the snow blotted out by a light bulb. That's too stupid. Well?' she then said.

'Well – do you want to hear more about Bakunin? About the International?'

'Yes. No. No, not now. When this is all over.'

She closed her eyes and began to sing softly. He didn't recognise the melody.

The rhythm of the train changed, it was braking. Anna peered out. 'Houses, all dark. Oh – a medieval wall. We entered a walled city.'

'Verona.'

'I hope he won't wake up.' She slowly raised the blind again.

The train stopped in a small station. The clock said ten minutes before two. The platform was almost empty, no passengers, a couple of railroad men. One, with a hammer, looked under the train but didn't touch it. Then another raised a little red flag. A whistle, and they pulled out. 'Two minutes in Verona. How stupid,' Anna muttered. She shielded her face against the glass with her hand, to see what it would look like after the station, but the train was immediately outside the town and running through fields that were black under the light sky. She lowered the blind.

Tolcheff looked meaningfully at her and said, 'There is a lady in Verona here, whom I affect; but she is nice, eh, I forgot that bit – nice lala, and nought esteems my aged eloquence,' and then began to laugh very hard.

She stared at him.

'Don't worry. A quotation. Ann, I wonder if you and I will ever make love again.'

'Oh, Tolcheff, what a question. When this is over. If it suits us.'

XXXII. Alpes-Maritimes (I)

The telegrams to 'Counsellor Zidkin (which Anna hadn't sent yet, as the train had only just left Verona and still had more than two hours to go to Milan) should have reached him neither at the Paris Embassy nor at the Hôtel du Parc in Cannes. For Zidkin was supposed to take the first train south from Paris on the day of Draskovich's scheduled arrival, the nineteenth. The 5.00 a.m. from the Gare de Lyon would have brought him into Cannes station in time to meet the Undersecretary.

The embassy would receive Anna's telegram at eight in the morning, by which time he would have long been gone. The Hôtel du Parc, where the other telegram would go, would never have laid eyes on him.

But when, on Monday of that week, Zidkin had wired the Hôtel du Parc to make the reservation for Draskovich, he had on the spur of the moment put 18 December instead of 19 December in his text.

Zidkin had ended up as a police liaison man only because once as a student he had successfully denounced some friends. He also didn't have the income for the regular diplomatic service. But his talent was administration, and he spent most of his time at the Paris Embassy on quiet lists and files in the consular section. He was an open-air-and-clean-living man, with diets and exercises, and no one knew him well. The secretary he worked with thought he was a nasty prig. When she read him the original Petersburg wire in which Draskovich requested his Cannes reservation and explained, with a considerable number of words, that it would be more convenient for him to have the Du Parc hotel as his headquarters during his legal mission with the Marseilles court, she had smiled. Zidkin had been furious. More convenient indeed. His room was to be booked in a commercial hotel across from the Marseilles railroad station. Zidkin hated Draskovich. As he might have to work under him one day in Petersburg, he had gone to such lengths not to show it that Draskovich thought Zidkin admired him greatly. Zidkin on his part had the mistaken idea that his services as a guide were appreciated by Draskovich whenever he came to France.

It was the smile of his secretary that had decided Zidkin in starting the hotel reservation a day early. No one would notice, no one in the embassy but he noticed that kind of thing. Instead of getting up at an ungodly hour on Wednesday, he would travel on Tuesday the eighteenth, have an evening by himself in Cannes, and a night in Draskovich's suite in the kind of hotel he had never stayed in.

Thus when Anna's train left Verona, Zidkin had just come back to the Du Parc hotel from an evening on the town, and after opening the mirrored wardrobe door in his bedroom half-way, he was for the first time in his life seeing himself from behind, in the large wall mirror. That sight dampened the euphoria created by the hundred francs he had won in the casino. He hadn't known that his chin receded that much when seen from a 120-degree angle, nor that he already had such a large b ld spot.

At that same hour of two in the morning, in the Hildesheimer Clinic in Super-Cannes, a mile to the north-east and five hundred feet above the Hôtel du Parc, the wounded Judge woke up. It was hot in his room and he felt uncomfortable. To his great relief, there was a glimmer of light at the edge of the curtains, and he assumed it was dawn. He pressed the bell and started counting, a game he always played, but at one hundred no one had come and he stopped. The morning nurse would be in soon.

The previous day, the doctor on his morning visit had told him he was definitely off their danger list, and he had been near weeping when he heard those words. He had felt a wave of sympathy and warmth towards himself, for seeing it through. Then, for the first time almost, he had started thinking about the Derkheim girl.

In the afternoon, when a Russian lady, a friend of a friend, came to sit by his bed to read to him, he had told her he wanted to dictate a memorandum.

It was addressed to the public prosecutor in Petersburg. As long as the Judge had felt he might die, he had forbidden himself to think about the legal aftermath of the attack. This was superstition: if he aimed at revenge instead of forgiveness, his wound might not heal and he might be doomed. But now he was free to pursue his thoughts. He informed the prosecutor, whom he knew personally, of course, that it was of the essence both for national prestige and for security, to get Derkheim extradited (he had not been told the machinery for that was already in motion). He mentioned a conspiracy in which the prosecutor, who had also dealt with Michael Derkheim, would be the next target. He stated that the girl had cried, 'We'll get you all.'

At that point he had broken off; he wanted more time to think up other cogent arguments. And his lady reader had been eager to go on with the book, a Guy de Maupassant novel.

He now lay thinking about this as he waited for the nurse. Other ideas for the memorandum would come to him. When he conjured up the picture of that girl with her big feet and her dripping raincoat, a loathing took hold of him and he knew that he must and would get the better of her.

The Judge looked again towards his window. But the light around the curtains had not grown stronger, it had gone. It must have been from some outside lamp. There had been light under the door; that had been turned off too. With dismay he realised that it wasn't morning. The night had only just begun. He listened for steps; no sound was audible but the beating of his heart.

He was afraid. He was on the verge of saying to himself, I'll forgive her. Instead of that, he crossed himself and whispered a prayer.

XXXIII. Verona-Milan

The railroad tracks now ran in an almost straight east–west line from the foothills of Lombardy to the city. With all signals favouring it, the express kept to a uniform speed of nearly seventy miles an hour. Between its huge head lamp and the red tail-lights, it was well-nigh dark. There was light in Draskovich's compartment where Tolcheff and Anna were sitting up and Draskovich was sleeping uneasily. A lamp was burning in the second restaurant car where the night conductor sat with his check list. The night waiter was dozing in the darkness of the kitchen corridor, in a wooden chair. No one had rung the bell for him since Vicenza.

All the passengers on the train then were satisfied or even satiated. After two and a half days of every beverage, or anyway every civilised European beverage at their command, plus Hungarian salami, caviar, Scottish salmon, prosciutto, Brie, Coulomiers, Camembert, Deux-Sèvres, Port Salut, Cantal, meringues, Amarettis, petits fours, pralines, Monte Cristo cigars, De Retzke cigarettes, there was nothing that any one of them felt like ringing for. All those delicacies were now rushed, unwanted, back to France, past unsatiated (but not hungry) farmhouses with ears of corn, much of it black-spotted at this time of the year, hanging in rows on the porches, and, as Milan drew nearer, past more and more industrialists' villas where equally satiated industrialists were sleeping, or worrying about tomorrow's Milan stock quotations, or perhaps making love. In the darkened compartments of the train there was little or no worrying, as most of their occupants had decided to leave that behind when they were going on their Riviera vacations. There was nothing to see except, if one opened one's eyes, a pleasantly simple and solid decor in the shimmer of the night light, and there was nothing to hear or to listen for but the perfectly regular rhythm of the wheels on the railroad ties. Most of the travellers were sexually at peace, too, except maybe for a very few who, alone or with incompatible companions, felt some desire or other they by themselves could not completely satisfy. All the others, in all their senses, were at rest. In this enclosed community flying along, freedom from want had temporarily been achieved, a Proundhonian utopia in which no one wanted for anything.

Further exceptions were Draskovich, who was licking his lips in his sleep from thirst, Anna and Tolcheff, who were still hungry as they had been for days, and the night conductor who, though within reach of all sorts of food, had looked very much forward to eating some of the leftover Lapereau Chasseur which had been on the menu that evening, and who had found to his disappointment and disgust that the cook had put the pot, with its lovely bottom of stew, under the cold tap.

XXXIV. Milan

At four fifteen in the morning, the express came to a halt in the Milan terminal, halfway down Platform 3. Anna, back in her black pumps once more, and clutching Tolcheff's watch, Draskovich's dispatch case and a ten-franc note that he had kept with his cigarettes, took only a second to orient herself. Then she was down the wide staircase, through the passenger tunnel, and up the stairs to Platform 1.

There wasn't a soul on it, no lighted sign, and she ran

first in one direction, then the other, before she saw the glass door with 'Posta'. But inside, quite a number of customers were coming and going through the opposite door, which opened on to the street. It was smoky, men were sitting on the bench along the wall with cigars and cigarettes and newspapers, others were writing at the stand-up desks. Everyone seemed wide awake and busy, a total transition to a remote world. How easy it would be to break away, to escape into another life, she thought. There is so much.

The windows showed a dark street, lit at the corner by a gas lamp.

Only one man was waiting at the telegraph counter, but he was holding a fistful of forms. When she made a sound of dismay, he looked around, lifted his felt hat, and offered, first in Italian and then in French, that the lady go first. She gave him a smile and pushed across the two identical telegrams to Zidkin, Paris, and Zidkin, Cannes, about Draskovich arriving a week later for personal reasons.

The clerk spoke to her, and when she did not immediately understand, he took two telegram forms from a pile and himself started copying out the texts which Tolcheff had written in French. He was fast enough: it was four twenty when he had completed this. He was clearly not the least concerned with their content or the identity of this Draskovich, but when he had done his sums, he asked her first for an amount in lire she didn't catch and then, looking at the money she held, for fourteen francs.

'Fourteen . . .' Anna repeated.

'It's the one-and-a-half rate, after midnight,' the man behind her said.

She stared at the telegrams and tried to figure out quickly how many words she'd have to skip. 'Personal' could go, and 'on', and 'Wednesday', and she put lines through those. The clerk looked less than happy and started counting again, while she tried to read the upside-down words, to take out more if needed. But she also kept looking at Tolcheff's watch and got into a kind of daze, in which she put a line through 'express' and then said, 'Oh, no, that stays.' At this point, the other customer said, 'Allow me, miss,' took the ten francs out of Anna's hand and, adding several liras, pushed it all across. 'Benissimo,' the clerk said, put the wires on the table behind him, and stamped two receipts for Anna.

'Well, thank you,' she said to the man in the felt hat.

He gave his forms to the clerk, and said, 'Perhaps you will take a coffee with me.'

He was rather heavy but not clumsy, with an outdoors face, in a worn but nice woollen overcoat. Like a ship's officer, she thought, or maybe a forester or a road engineer. Why would such a man send off a stack of telegrams in the middle of the night. Mystery.

'I'm wiring money to my associates,' he informed her.

'Oh? – I see.'

And she lost herself in an image dream. She was having a coffee with him in the station bar. They talked a long time, she had a nice feeling about him, it was all very simple. They came outside in the cold air of predawn. Anna's father had an enormous book with sketches of Rome by Ingres in his study; she had often leafed through it, and she now used it to see Milan. She could easily see the streets with their churches and palaces behind the gas lanterns. The man told her they should watch the sunrise over the city, from the balcony of his house, and she didn't object.

A silent courtyard, a stone staircase spiralling up, a tall door of light brown wood. They entered and walked through rooms with chairs under dust covers, he opened a french door, and they were on a balcony with a frail wrought-iron balustrade. The sun was just showing itself over a very distant row of trees. The streets lay quiet and limpid, and though they were in the heart of town, she heard the crowing of a rooster. A bedroom with a large bed under a baldachin, pull-up shutters, a few notes from a bird singing outside. No, no bird song in December. The floor was cold to her bare feet. His warm, tanned hands on her body, the sweet feeling of being entered, sweetly but irresistibly –

'I'm sorry, but I can't,' she said. She went to the platform exit, looked back once more with an apologetic shrug, and hurried down the stairs, through the tunnel, and up again.

'Task accomplished,' she told Tolcheff, as Draskovich, yawning, unshaven, and beginning to look the worse for wear, sat up in his corner and angrily stared from one to the other.

'Was it difficult?'

'No. They never questioned it.' She kicked off her shoes. The train pulled out. Draskovich began to laugh.

XXXV. Milan-Voghera

It was the behind-his-desk Draskovich again, she thought. 'You're a bunch of stupid fools,' he said, 'and you thought you were so smart. You,' (to Anna) 'I had put you down as being professional, in a fashion. And Andy the Fix, with his damn schoolmaster's manner – what a joke.'

'What exactly is the joke?' Tolcheff asked.

'You sent my wire to the Minister, to drop the extradition proceedings. You know what the wire says? I remember those things word for word, it says, "having taken full cognizance of local sensitivities and ramifications".'

He looked from one to the other. 'They still don't get it. You sent that from Milan! How stupid do you think we are? You saw through my Cannes post office plan, did you? And decided to beat me to it! What do you think Petersburg will do, when they read that? Local sensitivities – of the Milan stationmaster, I guess.'

'Oh.'

They acted perturbed, but perhaps not quite as perturbed as he had thought. Have they pulled a fast one? I wish my head was clearer. Draskovich enumerated all the plans they could possibly have made, though he didn't include the idea

hat they wouldn't have sent those wires he himself had
written for them, but others. That did not enter his mind.

It was of the essence to show them that he was still
needed. Otherwise there was no earthly reason why they
wouldn't kill him; in fact, what other guarantee could they
have that he wouldn't annul those messages? Why weren't
they more confused about their blunder? What were they
thinking?

'Maybe you figured, the Minister would think I had that
message sent from Milan to avoid the French laying eyes on
it,' he said.

'Maybe,' from Anna.

They looked as if they were about to burst out giggling.
They can't be planning my death. They're not that good,
they're amateurs, they'd be pale and shaky.

'There'd be something very strange about the timing,
wouldn't there now,' he said. 'They know I'm quick, but
not that quick.'

'Perhaps the Minister didn't keep such precise track of
your date of departure.' This from Tolcheff, very thoughtfully.

Fuck it. Quite true. Am I underestimating them? The
Minister wouldn't study it that precisely. 'I'm not a German,
I'm an artist,' he was fond of saying to his associates. 'Did
you put "3S" under it?' Draskovich then asked.

'Why? Wasn't that right?'

'Ha,' Draskovich answered. 'What do you think? A bit
too simple? 3S. Not much of a code, is it? You'd expect
something more subtle from the secret police. But then
again, who knows. To be simple is a virtue, too, at times.'

'We should torture him,' Tolcheff said to Anna, 'to get
the truth.'

'He's too fat. You do it.'

They are just damn amateurs. I'll be free and in Cannes
soon enough.

So let me think ahead. Can I simply countermand those
wires, from Cannes, and explain I was forced to send them?
Or, wait for a reaction first and then announce I don't know

anything about them? That's all a bit thin.

The right thing is to arrive a few days late, to explain was waylaid, was forced at gun point to send those tele grams, 3S code and all, and that I managed to free mysel That is good. Then I've turned this ridiculous affair int something positive. Plus, created a mood of indignation i which the French cannot refuse the request. Plus, a nic alibi for a nice long rest in Cannes. At bureau expense.

So. Get off the train, get them to take me off the train.

Not in France. Too tricky and too dangerous, the borde Get off while we're still in Italy. Room for manœuvre.

'All right,' he said slowly. 'It's time to put our cards o the table. I told you again and again, I'm no idealist, just businessman. No businessman wants a bullet in his stomac because there's an accounting error in his year report. That all that this means to me. Miss Anna is a bit too nervous fo my taste. I don't trust her with a pistol.'

'I won't shoot if I don't have to,' she said with assurance

'What you don't know is, I will be met. You were righ about that, of course. I am still an undersecretary after all.

'We never doubted it.'

'Yes, but not at Cannes station. I'm not your uncl coming on a Christmas visit. I'll be met by a French polic officer at the French-Italian border. That's protocol. An when he sees you, there'll be a shooting match, maybe. Wit me in the middle. And so, what I suggest is that you tw make yourselves scarce before that. You've got my chequ There must be a Crédit Lyonnais in Genoa, they're every where. You'll make out.'

'Just let go of you? With no guarantee?'

Draskovich shrugged. 'But there could never be an guarantee I couldn't break. Unless you kill me, which yo won't. Your guarantee is my vanity as a professional. I won want to announce that two muddleheads forced me to sen those wires. I told you that twice now. I'll uphold them. don't give a shit one way or the other. All I want now peace and quiet, and a good night's sleep without seeing yo two peering at me when I open my eyes.'

XXXVI. Voghera-Genoa (I)

The train did not stop at Voghera. Milan to Cannes: a long journey. One or two days by local trains perhaps. Once, she thought, when you had to go by stagecoach, at least a week or longer, through mountain passes, with mules down narrow roads, the abyss on one side, rocks, dark clouds over the moon. As you see on old prints. Not so very long ago. But now after this race from the end of Europe to its centre, it's only a final little jump. And with the express running faster and faster, like horses nearing their stable.

I am sentimental about this train. Sad. Nostalgic already. I haven't properly thought things out, the time has gone by too fast. This was my chance to get my life in a proper perspective.

That first morning after Petersburg, looking at myself, soaping my body, fields and houses flying by. I hadn't felt so happy in months or years. At home, there's never the occasion to look at yourself. No I don't mean, to look at yourself naked. The occasion to look at yourself from the outside, to stop the running of time, to stop this breathlessness. Breathlessness of unhappiness. To see yourself as a little figure on the surface of the earth, to understand, I am I. You'd think that'd be frightening, but it gives me peace.

I haven't completed this, I had wanted to become quite wise, quite at peace.

But then, we'll have to go back, too. That would be an undeserved boon, another three days and nights on this train, without Draskovich.

We're obviously not going to do what Draskovich suggests. Even if it's true that it's nothing to him, he'd be too spiteful to let us win our case. It'd be funny, of course, if he made a big thing out of denying those two telegrams we haven't even sent. Maybe he's lying again, about that escort at the border. It's one of those puzzles, he may say it because then we'll think it's not true and then we'll think it's true because he wants us to think it's not true and so on and so forth. We can't risk it, that's the long and the short of it. Tolcheff and I must get him off at Genoa. As we half planned already.

There wasn't even any need for a whispered discussion about it with Tolcheff. He had silently formed the word 'Genoa', and she had nodded.

We are in a sort of harmony, he and I. Not like lovers, as he tries to make it. Like brother and sister. Like my brother. An older brother. Older? I'm not sure.

Anna had had a brother, five years younger than she. He had died when he was three and a half. She rarely thought of him, but she remembered him very well. His name was – for one frightening moment she couldn't say his name. His name was Boris. 'We're going to have an ABC of children, your mother and I,' her father had told her. But there hadn't been any others.

Boris, what a pretentious name for such a little creature, its weight would have worn him out. She had always called him B, for baby. Such a death should have shaken the world, why should its bitterness be any less than for a ship lost in a storm or armies fighting a battle? Nobody's mourning can take in a hundred dead. But she hadn't been allowed to miss even one day in school or to go to his funeral. Had her parents been right about that? Now the last thing she could recall was him looking at her, with his quiet, puzzled eyes. Poor little rat. But it makes no difference in a hundred years. Screw it all.

XXXVII. Voghera-Genoa (II)

Draskovich's main sensation now was discomfort. This train started so pleasantly, he thought, and then it got spoiled. Serves me right, I was getting too damn smug. I'll make up for it in France, though. I wonder how warm the weather will be there. January can be so nice on the Côte.

I think I played it right. Those two will force me off the train in Genoa, or that's how it will look to them. I'll sit it out quietly, and get away when I really want to. They'll run out of steam soon enough. Maybe they'll even take my lead and go off by themselves. Then I'll lie low for a day or two in a really first-class hotel, before going on to Cannes. A hot bath, clean sheets.

Yes, I didn't handle it too badly. But I'm not very clear-headed all the same, and the reason is that I'm so damn dirty and tired, dying to get out of these clothes, to have an undisturbed shit. In a war I'd be a fine officer and a lousy private. I'm no coward, but I can't think properly when I don't have my creature comforts. I can't be cool and collected when I'm sweaty and haven't been to the toilet in a day.

Perhaps there's a lesson in that to break down people.

I've always hated beatings and fingernails and all that stuff. They think I'm cruel but I hate it. They don't realise we don't do things to make people suffer or to make them confess something. Confess. That is medieval. We don't need to hear some bugger confirm that we were right. We are after answers, information. Everyone in the world does it. They tell me, England. Well, I don't know. If there's one country that doesn't, that would only mean they're so strong, so hopelessly on the winning end, that they don't need to. You'd be worse off than with us, in a place like that, if you were in trouble. Every government needs to know everything everyone knows, and more. Nothing inhuman, very human. Animals have no need to question each other, ha ha.

But perhaps discomfort is as good as pliers. Maybe the simple and civilised way is just to have them stay awake or sleep in their clothes for one or two hours only, watch them when they try to shit, prevent them from washing, small things. Wet feet. Noise. Silence. Perhaps that would be enough to deheroise those heroes. Try to be a hero with snot running down your face, shit in your pants.

Petrov would be disappointed. Petrov is a simple case of course, he's some kind of sex pervert. 'I just tore him open in the end,' that's what he told me of that fellow last week. We should at least have machines, electricity, Leyden jars or something. Petrov makes me sick. I have to get rid of that man. Arrange it in a roundabout way, I don't want him as my enemy. First thing, though, when I'm back.

But when I'm honest with myself, I admit I understand him. There's something voluptuous about it, no denying that. I don't give in to it, because I'm a gentleman. But otherwise . . . Maybe even for the victim, perhaps the first split second of being stretched on the rack was sensual. Didn't Petrov tell us, when you hang a man, he has an erection? Petrov's a moron, though. Probably an automatic reaction. No pleasure. Not worth it, ha ha.

Only don't tell me the people are good, Mr Tolcheff. The people would flock to hangings the way we go to the ballet, twentieth century or no twentieth century. Nothing has changed.

Robert Damiens. The madman who attacked Louis Fifteen with a penknife. Hardly touched him. And the good King convened a meeting of the leading anatomists of Paris, and they all came, and they deliberated just precisely what tortures would keep Damiens alive longest and make him suffer and scream most. And the good people of Paris, those

great revolutionaries, had a ball, trampled each other under-
foot for a better look. Imagine that scene, a half-crazy guy
screaming, and his fellow citizens, his barber and baker,
gaping at him and shivering and grinning.

What a disgusting tribe we are. What a heritage. Maybe
that was all they had going for them, though. They needed
Damiens to see someone more miserable than themselves
and to have emotions besides cold and hunger. I wonder how
he looked. Like Tolcheff maybe. Thin, hungry. Poor devil,
really. Pain. Crime. All quite mysterious. Where's the room
in your body for all that pain. Our good Czar Ivan just used
boiling and ice-cold water. As effective probably. The
capacity to feel pain can't be endless. There must be a border
you reach any old way. Of course, that fellow had struck
the King. Like striking God to them. There's a neat defini-
tion of crime, a crime is whenever a man or a woman
doesn't lie low, tries to disturb the natural order of things.
I can use that. It's like putting your hand in a flywheel. Of
course, the result is bloody, you can't expect it not to be.

Still, they're pathetic in the end. For I guess the natural
order could have ended up looking quite different. But it
didn't. Not my fault . . .

He had a strange, novel feeling that he was sorry for
everyone. Everyone, except himself.

I am one man who knows exactly what he is doing.

XXXVIII. Voghera-Genoa (III)

The intense awareness of her body near his.

Their plan had taken a turn, they were no longer drifting.
Some kind of control had been regained. Tolcheff experienced that idea as a deliverance – but, to his bewilder-

ment, all different from what he had expected till then. His relief was about Draskovich-Sophia no longer looming so large, about being able to concentrate on Ann without guilt feeling. And with that came a desire for her, that swept over him; but it's all true, he thought, the clichés in naughty novels, about floods and storms and seas of passion. But I'm not dreaming of getting her to a secluded little villa on the bay in Peterhof.

At least not that.

She will be my companion from now on. He would wander through Europe, hunted perhaps, secretly, but with her. They would escape from police together, address strikers, travel in disguises. At night they'd fall in each other's arms, sometimes soaked with rain, freezing, only needing warmth and softness. And then again they would make love in barns on the straw, in abandoned ruins, on the bottom of a rowboat floating, unseen by patrols, down a river.

Like Garibaldi and his wife, that young girl from Brazil. What was her name.

He looked at Anna, but just then her face was so sad and vulnerable that he hastily turned his eyes away.

It's more than wanting her; for I can't bear her being vulnerable. And that's precisely when she'd be most open, most easily had. Literally.

Enough of this sloppy introspection. No more bodies stuff.

When Tolcheff wanted to discipline his thoughts, as he called it, he started to draft pamphlets in his head. Class war.

Three classes everywhere.

One, the usurpers. Why? People were equal once. The usurpers convinced us of their greater rights.

Second class, the cowards. They're the occupied country. Precisely. Take France in the 1870 war. The Prussians are the usurpers. The middle class, the bourgeois, are the cowards. When the attack begins, they're waiting in line.

Not to enlist, not to escape even, but at the savings bank and at the grocer's. Perhaps you can't blame them too much, but there's no cause for applause, that's for sure.

The third class are the rebels, the Commune. Always the same. some of the poor, some half intellectuals like me, some real fighters, men like Garibaldi.

These could just possibly, miraculously, win. But the cowards are so scared of trouble that they hate the rebels for not accepting the situation. And then, they get convinced by the usurpers that all is well. It is. No one is touching their savings accounts after all.

That was country country war. Now it is the war of all against all. It is harder to see, the fights are underground. It is the same division and every country has its Prussians.

And Draskovich? He's in a sub-group. A mercenary of the usurpers. If he does well, he becomes one of them. That's how most of them started, of course, going right back to knighthood. At least he's not one of the cowards. Conceivably then he could also become a mercenary for us? What? Well, he was good at Pontebba, he didn't stir a muscle.

Oh, come now, Tolcheff. That was police dog courage, they hang on, too.

But Drasky is not a dog, he is my fellow man.

Perhaps I have been wrong to treat him with contempt. If I'd shown him a palpable feeling, of what, of brotherhood? Held out my hand to him, like a brother? Stop all that smart-alecky stuff, Draskovich, all those facts-of-life, remember that you are a mortal man –

His thoughts drifted. Righting the wrongs of all centuries, of all history.

He saw an enormous building, like the Crystal Palace in London but ten times larger. In it, floors, departments, rooms, the rooms with counters like a giant post office. Everyone. Everyone would come in for a final settling of all injustice. For instance. A child would be directed to the Religion Department, Catholic Church floor, window ES-1674, the Seville auto-da-fé of 1674. 'Yes?' the priest behind the window asks. My great-great-great-grandfather was burned at the stake there. The boy shows the card from the central filing system he had received. They look up the tears shed, the lost years. The priest offers the child a thousand pounds sterling, to go to the university and become the scholar the burned heretic was. Or, if he doesn't want that, the priest will come out from behind his window, follow him home, and for ten years perform the boy's household chores which his mother makes him do and which he hates so.

Long lines at all those windows, mostly the poor, the descendants of victims, English peasants chased off their land and then hanged for tramps, Russian peasants made serfs, Indians, Africans, Jews, Irishmen. Some well-dressed others. A few would want to send their lawyers to stand in line for them but we wouldn't have that.

And behind the windows, the rich and mighty would sit, the descendants of victimisers, and succeed one another as each took up a task of retribution.

Where would I be, in the line, or behind a window through my father's blood, blood of a slaver perhaps or of a judge? What a frightening word, to *judge* your fellow men on this planet, equally lost with you. Better be in the line.

A secular Judgement Day, that's what I cooked up here. Bus isn't it better for human dignity if we do it ourselves? If we ourselves draw a line under our terrible history?

What about victims without descendants? They're probably the majority, dying without a ripple. Without a trace left of their earthly existence. But at least no one would go on profiting *now*, visibly.

The dead, and the sick, children born with crippled bodies – there'll be enough left for God's Judgement Day. If it's still scheduled.

He raised the blind. There was a glimmer of light in the sky, the night was almost at its end.

Draskovich was sleeping. Anna stared fixedly ahead, but holding her little pistol in a solid grip.

Dawn. Dawn, a party in an Italian walled garden which had lasted through the night. Musicians playing on a terrace, coloured lights under the trees. A stone pavilion over a pond in a far corner of the grounds, near the old wall, away from the other guests. A young woman sitting opposite him. She asks, who are you, I know you weren't invited, none of our people talks as you talked to me this night. And I answer, I have to leave before it gets light. Why? Because I have to. Why? I must know. Because of the police, the men in the tricorn hats, I escaped from their dungeons. I will hide you in my room, kiss me. He bends over her. She is Ann. Of course she is Ann. Draskovich and his sensualities. The women in the open carriages along the sea boulevard, soft, open, like sea anemones. To give in to that. But Ann is hard and thin and there is more sensuality in that, in making love to her, endlessly more, than in those white, yielding bellies that gently enclose you, gently female serve you. Draskovich wouldn't understand that. He's just a fucker. At least he offered five thousand francs. Not everyone gets an offer from the devil. I guess only if they're sure you won't accept.

The light in the sky was more than a glimmer now. A single cloud, ow over the western horizon, stood out against the blackness, touched by a reflection of colour from the east which he could not see.

The sky was turning from black to a dark blue, and a jagged line of real blackness was traceable in it. The Ligurian mountains. Liguria. I could travel through names, through words only.

Putting the Webley in his right-hand pocket – just for one moment – he stuck his head out of the window, his eyes closed against the enormous wind from the train which slapped in his face, turning his head away from it, breathing in the cold morning air.

XXXIX. Genoa, the railroad station

Now rocky slopes and ravines became visible, a wild and
desolate landscape; then, whoosh, a tunnel. Tolcheff hastily
closed the window against the smoke. A narrow stone platform ran between the train and the wall, and every hundred
feet or so an electric lamp made the wet inside of the
mountain glitter.

Anna shook herself, smiled at him, and put her shoes
back on. The different noise of the train woke up Draskovich,
who grunted and rubbed his eyes.

The tunnel seemed endless, they could feel the air click in
their ears and there was a rising uneasiness between them.
Then with another whoosh like a cork out of a bottle, they
were in the open again. It was fast growing lighter. The
slopes were covered with grapevines here, villas appeared
amidst groves and along white, pebbled roads.

'Genoa,' Draskovich said. They entered another tunnel,
daylight for a second, and still another one; they raced
through a small depot and turned a wide left curve. Left,
we're turning east, Tolcheff thought, how's that, we must
have reached the seacoast. But all he could see from the
window now was a bare hillside, little fields with walls built
of stones, a goat, dilapidated huts. Over it a low sky,
weighing down on the land: the day had not preserved the
clarity of dawn. Then they were back in another tunnel, the
train braked and entered the Genoa railroad yards. A vast
terrain of tracks and hangars and cinders, and over it a
scattered cloud of electric lights, still burning and making
the day seem even murkier.

Anna and Tolcheff stood up.

'Put your coat on, Drasky,' Tolcheff said. 'We're getting off here. Just to be on the safe side.'

Draskovich looked blank, he got into his coat without a word and waited.

The train came to a halt. The shock made Draskovich sit down, but he immediately stood up again. The platform outside was quiet, with a small group of travellers, and a cart selling newspapers, fruits, and little bottles of liqueurs. Tolcheff lowered the window and cried, 'Portabagaglil' looking rather pleased with himself as he did. He said to Anna, 'Don't you agree it's better to get his things out of here, so they don't find them in Cannes? Would you hand them to the porter?'

She went behind him to the window, and he motioned Draskovich to get out into the corridor. He stayed close behind him, the dispatch case under his left arm and pointing the Webley, inside his jacket pocket.

On the platform outside the car door stood an attendant, who saluted Draskovich with a surprised air. Draskovich nodded back and walked on; Tolcheff nodded, too, and followed, like an assistant trailing his boss. If he runs, I'd shoot, he thought with satisfaction, I'd shoot and get away in that crowd here. For towards the end of the platform a local train was waiting to depart, with a great press of people and a din of voices and bells of luggage carts.

Behind him, Anna handed the suitcases through the window to the porter. He looked startled at their lack of weight and asked her something. She smiled at him and said, 'Si, si, benissimo.'

When she was out on the platform, she could still see Draskovich and Tolcheff ahead. Half-way down towards the exit was the window of the left-luggage room, and she pointed at it. The porter nodded, and gave her a metal number for a receipt. She hurried after the others, but before reaching them, she stood still and looked over her shoulder. She made a fluttery movement with her hand, as if she were brushing something from her cheek: she was waving good-bye to her train.

XL. Genoa, the town

At the exit gate Draskovich seemed to hesitate, but then he took out the cigarette case and gave the controller his ticket, which he had kept in there. Anna glanced at Tolcheff, who didn't look back: he should have foreseen this, and got hold of it before. He only had his own ticket and Anna's. He hastily produced them.

At the adjacent entrance, a stream of people was coming in, but the three of them stood alone at the exit, facing the controller, who was sitting on a little chair outside his booth and who took his time studying their tickets. Ahead lay a long and rather narrow passage; they could hear the noise of the traffic now but they could not see the street. They looked at Draskovich. Impossible to guess what he was thinking.

'Convalidare?' the controller asked and when neither Tolcheff nor Anna answered, Draskovich said 'Si, per favore. He asks us if we want our tickets validated for the unused part,' he informed them pleasantly. 'We may as well, don't you think?'

They came outside and faced a square teeming with traffic, a greyish, dusty city morning. Anna was bewildered. All those ideas of mine, it doesn't look that different from Petersburg. Then a moment of fear: plans made in a train compartment that had to be translated into this enormous reality of tall buildings, carriages, carts, and trucks rattling by over the uneven pavement, hurrying men and women. Tolcheff felt the same, or perhaps he was disconcerted by Draskovich's casual manner, for he took him by the arm in a new, rough fashion and steered him away from the crowd and into a silent little side street.

'That's it, the worst is over,' he assured Anna. 'The station was the tricky part.'

Draskovich freed his arm and brushed his jacket sleeve. 'Do you have to march me along like a gangster?' he asked.

'Come on.' Tolcheff said, 'this way.' He had a plan and he knew approximately which direction to take. Tolcheff took Draskovich's arm again and Anna stayed half behind, occasionally poking him with her pistol through her coat. 'It's nice to stretch one's legs, isn't it?' Draskovich remarked. 'But I'd like a shave, and some breakfast, if that's part of the plan.'

'Later.'

Tolcheff tried to lead them in an easterly direction, continuing the way they had come in on the train. turning a corner whenever the road ahead seemed busy. It was a silent part of town, though, of neglected houses and empty apartment buildings about to be torn down for an extension of the rail yards. Garbage was strewn everywhere. and Anna had trouble keeping up on the sharp cobblestones. They passed a porter pushing a wheelbarrow, and Tolcheff asked, without stopping, 'Via Lanzio?'

They didn't understand his answer, but his gestures seemed to indicate a street nearby, to the right. They turned the corner the man pointed at, and came out on to an asphalted road, with large and sombre houses on one side, and a factory behind a high fence, amidst fields overgrown with weeds, on the other.

'This is it,' Tolcheff said. 'Via Lanzio. Soon, Ann.'

They went on and, after passing an abandoned building site, came to a narrow stone house, four storeys high, its façade, once red, now a blackish sepia.

Tolcheff pointed.

The street windows of the building were all shuttered; above its entrance door, along the second floor, ran a balcony with an empty flagstaff. A wooden sign was tied to the railing with ropes, and on it was painted, 'Edificio Unità. Partito Socialista Italiano.'

Tolcheff gave Draskovich a little push with the pistol, which he had taken out of his pocket. 'Go in,' he said.

He turned to Anna. 'Here we will be with friends.'

XLI. Genoa, Via Lanzio

They came into a dark entrance hall where there was no one. The tiled floor had a faded mosaic; against one wall stood a worn black leather bench. Small half-circle windows let in the only light. Anna tried several doors until she found one unlocked.

It led her into a room that was bare except for a kitchen table and chair. A young man was standing in front of the table, sorting out a pile of mimeographed papers. A window in the rear saw out on a courtyard where crates were piled around a dry stone fountain with a moss-covered stone frog sitting on top, its mouth wide open. Anna smiled at the young man and asked if he spoke French, or English. He held up a finger as a sign for her to wait and hurried off, returning with an older man in a blue seaman's sweater, who asked in English, 'Yes, lady?'

'We are here on a party mission,' she said. 'From Russia. We must see the party secretary, or someone like him.'

'We?'

She beckoned him to follow and took him out into the entrance hall. The seaman began to smile, but then stood still with some consternation as he took in Tolcheff with his pistol and briefcase, and Draskovich in his smoking jacket under his open, fur-collared coat. He hastily turned and left the hall, catching the young man, who was just coming in too, by the arm and taking him out again with him.

'That got action,' Anna said. Draskovich yawned and

suggested they sit down. 'Go ahead,' from Tolcheff.

Another door opened and several men came in, trailed by the seaman. They were all in neat dark suits, their shirts were closed at the neck with studs but without the detachable collars. They looked so different from what Anna had expected that she gave Tolcheff a conspiratorial smile. He didn't notice, he was shaking hands with one of the men who told him in English that he was the Genoa party secretary.

'We are very happy to meet with you,' Tolcheff said. 'This is Anna, a friend, and this is our prisoner.'

'Perhaps we better all go up to the office,' the secretary suggested, pointing the way.

Everyone trooped up a narrow stone staircase, Draskovich with the empty look on his face first, then Anna, Tolcheff, and the secretary, and all the others following behind.

The office seemed to cover most of the top floor and looked out over the factory and the fields. From up here, the wind could be seen to weave strange patterns in the high weeds. The strong light from the glittery sky showed every crack in the ceiling, the pieces of cardboard propping up the legs of desks, the brown stains on the wall where there must have been a washbasin once. And Anna felt her heart sink because of this poverty which here, more than in the slums of Petersburg, seemed so much within the natural order of human life, against which all those books and pamphlets piled high everywhere seemed so powerless.

They sat down. Those who couldn't find a chair posted themselves in the window sills.

'Now then, friends,' the secretary said in English, after he had installed himself behind a desk.

Tolcheff was the only one who had remained standing. He went over to the secretary and said, 'I'd like a word in private with you.' The two went out on to the landing from where the murmur of their voices could be heard.

It remained silent in the office, until Draskovich announced in the British-sounding English he had cultivated, 'I would appreciate a cigarette.' Everyone looked at him, and then his neighbour handed him a cigarette and gave him a light. After that, they all stared out of the window or studied their nails or their shoes, but whenever Anna caught a man's eyes, he gave her a shy smile.

When the two had come back, the secretary, once more behind his desk, seemed uncertain what to say. Tolcheff declined the chair which someone, getting up, offered him and went to sit on the window sill.

At that point, Draskovich got to his feet. 'Perhaps I'll have my say now,' he said, speaking to the secretary only, 'to save embarrassment later. The matter between me and these two, eh, overenthusiastic young people, is entirely outside your concern. But here I am, a Russian government official, brought at gun-point to your premises. I realise you were taken by surprise. You must now take immediate measures to remedy the situation, and then I on my part will consider the incident closed. I think you realise that this young man here, with his gangster pistol, is hazarding the existence of your party with his rashness.'

Anna looked at Tolcheff, who shrugged. No one spoke. Then the secretary got up again and shepherded two other men out on to the landing for a consultation. After a few minutes, he appeared in the doorway and beckoned Tolcheff to join them. Those left behind in the office started to talk among themselves in low voices. Shortly thereafter, the others came back in.

The secretary sat down once more, rummaged in a drawer, and began to speak, looking from Tolcheff to Anna and back. 'Unfortunately – We have no choice but to follow the suggestion from this gentleman. We apologise to our friend from Russia, Andrea Tolcheff, and his young lady. This year 1900 has been a year of crisis for our party. The Pirelli strike in Milan was broken by the army, with artillery. The paper, *La Critica Sociale*, was banned. Many are in prison.' His eyes went around the room. 'Sir,' (to Draskovich) 'of course you can leave. We must apologise to you.'

Draskovich didn't look triumphant. He got up, brushed his coat, and went to shake hands with the secretary. 'I trust,' he said, 'that you will see to it that those two cannot follow me hot foot.' He pronounced it as two separate words.

'We can hardly keep them prisoners.'

'If that is the case, I will insist that the police are called before I leave.'

'Oh, never mind,' Tolcheff said. 'We won't follow you.'

Draskovich nodded. He went over to Anna and she imagined he meant to shake hands with her, too. She got up, clutching the pistol in her coat pocket. He stopped a few feet away from her and holding out his hand, said, 'My luggage receipt, if you please.' Tolcheff took a step towards them, but Draskovich didn't look around at him.

It was deadly quiet in the room now.

She stared at Tolcheff's face. Pain – she felt a general pain all over her body, undefined, as of a beating. His expression didn't change, showed nothing.

Then she let go of the pistol and brought out the luggage number. Draskovich took it, picked up his dispatch case, which Tolcheff had put on a desk, bowed vaguely towards the company, and was gone. His measured steps could be heard on the stone stairs.

Tolcheff went over to her and put his hand on her shoulder, but she made an involuntary gesture to shake it off.

'I've got the papers from his briefcase in my pocket,' he said to her.

'Oh, Andrew Tolcheff – ' she began, stamped her foot, turned her back on him, and went to look out of the window.

Tolcheff glanced at the other men, then he pulled out his handkerchief, one of Draskovich's, and wiped his forehead with it. It was yellow silk with a dark red edge, and as he saw their eyes on it, he gave a little laugh.

The Italians got up and left the room, conversing in undertones. The secretary said, 'I'll be back. I'll get you two some bread and coffee.'

XLII. Genoa, Via Roma

As Draskovich left the Unità building behind him he made
a point of neither hurrying nor smiling. There was no one to
see him, but that was the way an English gentleman would
behave. He breathed in the air with a pleasure he felt he had
earned. God, how many hours had it been? An eternity, with
those two. Later I'll analyse my moves. First get out of this
neighbourhood, and into that hot bath.

In the next street, he came upon an empty cab pulled up
in front of a horse butcher. He looked in and found the
coachman, a shabby fellow in sandals, watching intently as
the butcher weighed him a piece of bluish meat on a scrap of
newspaper. He turned away, but the man had noticed him
and called out, 'One second, here I come.'

Draskovich told him to drive to the railroad station first,
where he sent him in to collect his suitcases; from there he
went to the Hotel Isotta on Via Roma. He had never stayed
in Genoa, but the Isotta had been mentioned to him.

The hotel, with its heavy dark blue porte-cochère, was as
smart as he had hoped. He told the doorman to pay the fare;
he avoided even looking at his driver. The sight of that man,
with the package of horse meat sticking out of the breast
pocket of his jacket, on which the outline of a bloodstain
seemed to appear, filled him with disgust.

At the desk, he asked for a suite with a private bathroom.
And while the receptionist checked the list, as Draskovich
stood idly staring out into the street, he saw that the coachman was still there. The fellow seemed to have waited to
catch his eye, and now lifted his hat to him in apparent mock
gratitude. Doormen probably don't tip very well, Draskovich

thought, they need to make their own profit on it.

That little reflection suddenly filled him with a sense of well-being. He was on his own again, he had walked out from under an armed threat, and was turning a preposterous mishap into a creditable adventure. He was waited on, in this vast, warm, brightly lit marble lobby, while outside in the grey street two other men, men like him, were at odds over ten or twenty centesimi. I'm doing all right, as far as going through life on earth is concerned.

He now became aware of a certain commotion behind him, and a bell captain came up to the counter and whispered to the receptionist.

'I beg your pardon,' the receptionist said. 'But it seems, eh, that your suitcases are all empty. Under the circumstances, you will agree – '

'What!' shouted Draskovich. He jerked a portmanteau out of the hands of a bellboy, put it on the counter, and opened it. 'I'll be damned. Those little hoodlums. The bloody thieves.' But where could they have hidden the stuff? How could she have had time to take it all out and where could she have put it? He reconstructed the scene on the railroad platform. It was impossible.

His anger and bafflement had their effect on the hotel. There were now two receptionists behind the counter, and Draskovich's reaction switched them from thinking he was a hotel crook to worry that the loss would be ascribed to Genoese thievery. 'I'm sure, sir,' one of them began, 'that the police – '

'Never mind,' Draskovich interrupted. He had looked in his dispatch case and seen that the chequebooks were there. 'I've been robbed, but I'll pursue it later. All I want now is my bath and some sleep. And please have breakfast sent up, and, yes, you'd better send out for a pair of pyjamas in my size.'

'Certainly, sir. I will take down your order myself.'

'I will have . . .' Draskovich considered the various possibilities with leisurely contentment. 'I will have baby lamb chops, grilled. Whatever you have in fresh fruits at this time of the year. Some good cheese. A bottle of Vichy, coffee of course, and yes, perhaps some little champagne, very dry, just a split.'

'Immediately,' both receptionists said, their doubts over Draskovich having evaporated.

XLIII. Alpes-Maritimes (II)

The French postal service, excellent from as far back as the days of Napoleon, had delivered the Milan telegram for Zidkin at his Cannes hotel before seven that morning. and it was taken up straight away to Draskovich's suite where Zidkin was spending the night.

Zidkin had only gone to bed at two, and when he saw it was Draskovich who even at a distance prevented him from sleeping late, he muttered a for him unusual oath.

'Counsellor Zidkin.' Zidkin was only a Third Secretary of Embassy, and that address embittered him still more. It was a typical Draskovich joke, he felt, nasty without it being clear exactly why. Somehow it seemed to convey Draskovich's conviction that he would never make it to counsellor.

But when the contents of the message had sunk in, all that was forgotten. 26 December! He had a week by himself, seven days he could stay in this suite, draw a per-diem maybe, and do as he pleased. He considered for a moment whether he was supposed to go back and wait in Paris, but dismissed that. Draskovich didn't say so in his telegram, and that covered him. He reread it several more times. 'Personal reasons' – no doubt one of Draskovich's doubtful affairs. And '3S', what did that mean? Zidkin felt uneasily in the presence of another of Draskovich's little jokes, a kind of test of his perception, which he knew he would fail. Three what? What started with S? Three signorinas? That could quite possibly be it, Draskovich in pseudo cipher explaining those personal reasons and announcing that he had shacked up in Milan with three girls. He used to go on like that in Paris with me, too. What a disgusting man, what is he trying to prove? But, till Wednesday, to hell with him.

Zidkin was now wide awake. He got himself ready in a hurry and went downstairs. The lobby was being swept by two women, and the receptionist was drinking a cup of coffee which he put out of sight when he saw Zidkin come down the stairs. Zidkin nodded at him. I must tell him and I must send some wires about Draskovich, to the embassy and to the police in Menton, or they'll go meet the train. Later. He walked out over the front lawn, through the main gate, and found himself face to face with the Mediterranean.

Having arrived the evening before on the Paris train, he hadn't yet seen Cannes by day. It was a lovely morning; the sky was of a soft, almost springtime, blue; the sun, rising just beyond the line of the boulevard, above the sea, threw a long line of light over the little waves. The water was so pure that you'd think you'd be able to breath in it, Zidkin thought, to live on the bottom of this bay. This is perfection, the perfect weather, the non-weather, you're not aware there is an atmospheric condition whose peculiarities must be discussed. It is like being in heaven.

He surprised himself, I'm not that lyrical or intense usually.

This is my habitat. I should have been born French. I understand this country better than my own. How does that song go, 'Je cherche fortune . . .'

He went down the steps from the boulevard to the beach. He was humming, taking vast strides, determined not to let a second of his time go untasted.

XLIV. Genoa (departure)

They washed, and Tolcheff shaved, in the little bathroom of
the Unità building, taking turns under a tap only dripping
bits of water. They had their bread and coffee, and shook
hands with the secretary, who looked rather stricken and
who, with his arm around Tolcheff's shoulder, whispered
things in his ear he didn't understand, and who insisted on
lending or giving them three scudi, fifteen lire. Then they
went back to the station.

It was only ten when they got there. 'It's as if a day has
gone by,' Anna said. They studied the schedules, the next
through train to Nice, where they'd have to change for
Cannes, was leaving at 12.31 p.m., due in Nice at 8.15 that
evening. They looked at the board for a while, without
discussing whether Draskovich could be expected to take
that train, or what they would now do in Cannes. Turning
around, they walked silently back into town.

'Look,' he said. On the far corner of the station square
stood a building with, in golden letters, 'Crédit Lyonnais.'

'Let's try,' they both said at the same moment.

They had to take a number for their turn, and then there
was a long wait. Several times they were on the point of
leaving; suppose Draskovich had warned the bank or the
police?

'I can't cash this cheque,' the clerk at the window said.
'For this particular account, two signatures are required.'

'Two? Of whom?' Anna asked.

'I'm not at liberty to discuss that,' the clerk answered,
suspiciously eyeing them as he shoved the cheque back and
forth in front of him. 'But I better make a report about this.'

'No, no,' Anna told him. 'I'm Mr Draskovich's secretary. I'm sure there's a mistake somewhere.' She gave him her most complicated smile, while Tolcheff edged himself out of the field of vision.

'Well, the mistake isn't here,' the clerk said, slightly more friendly.

'No, of course not. My boss is a very forgetful man, I'm sure he just – I'll take it back to him.' And she snatched the cheque back from under the bars.

Her smile had worked. 'Come back to this window, miss,' the clerk now said, 'and you won't have to stand in line again.'

'Damn,' Tolcheff said outside.

'We could have known. Drasky. Look, there are even two lines here for signatures.'

'Don't tear it up, Ann,' he asked. 'We'll think of something, maybe.'

They wandered through the busy streets, a bit furtively as the shadow of Draskovich hung over the town. By silent consent they didn't stop in front of stores or buy food with their lire, but kept walking at a fast clip, as if they were being followed.

A winding alleyway, with steps of black lava stones at its steepest places, led them up the hillside which cradled the harbour. Laundry waved from one side to the other, thin children played in the gutters. They went more slowly now, for this was not a spot where you'd run into Draskovich. At the top they came to a little park with short brown grass, facing a church. They sat down on a bench; Anna announced her feet were hurting.

An old man came over to them from the next bench, a frighteningly decrepit figure with black stumps for teeth and brown snot or blood dripping from his nose, a greenish white skin showing through rents in his waistcoat. Tolcheff only had the three five-lire pieces and he held up his hands in a gesture of regret. Anna rumbled in her pocketbook and couldn't find anything but her watch. 'It's about had it, anyway,' she muttered and gave it to the man.

He accepted it with a trembling hand and shuffled away under the bare trees, crossed over, and entered the gate of a barracks with little barred windows.

'He's going to sell it to the soldiers. Good.'

Tolcheff stood up to see better. 'That's no barracks, that's where he lives. It says "Albergo de' Poveri", the poorhouse.'

'Oh. I hope they won't steal it from him.' She frowned and looked away.

'Me in thirty years,' Tolcheff said.

As he sat down again beside her, the church clock behind them struck eleven.

They turned to each other, and at the same moment got up and started down the little street. They had been going in a circle before; now rushing back, they found themselves in the station square when it was still only eleven fifteen.

'Let's take that train,' Tolcheff said and she nodded. They hurried to its platform and waited there, although they had more than an hour to go, and when the train had been formed at noon, they immediately boarded it. Tolcheff steered them to a third-class carriage where a conductor, with the same facial expression the bank clerk had used earlier, informed them their tickets were valid for first class.

Thus they were sitting alone in a compartment, green velvet this time, of a carriage with not a single other passenger, across from each other, taking turns in peering out of the window, fearing and hoping that Draskovich would appear on the platform.

When finally the minute hand of the station clock jumped to thirty-one and the train got into motion with a violent lurch forward and backward and forward again, they began to smile.

'Hurrah, Ann. We're off again.'

'Not quite as smoothly as the Petersburg Express.'

'Ah – nothing is.'

'Alone,' she added.

'Thank heaven. And we'll beat him to it.'

'To what?' she asked.

'I'll show you.' And he emptied the pockets of the tweed jacket he was wearing, and spread the contents beside him: the pistol, shaving things, bread left over from the Unità, and the drafts of the Draskovich telegrams. 'Don't laugh,' he said. 'But here's a plan of mine. No, why are you smiling?'

'Not because of your plans, I love your plans,' Anna answered. 'I was thinking of Drasky and his empty suitcases, his face.'

'You should have seen all that stuff. It's gone back to the people. Christmas presents from the secret police.'

'I wonder where he is, Andrew. Wouldn't it be lovely if he had got stuck or arrested?'

'Undersecretary Draskovich? Never. He's asleep in a large expensive hotel bed.'

And so he was.

XLV. Genoa-San Remo

At Pegli, emerging from a tunnel, they saw the sea.

The sky was still overcast here, and the water was blue grey, with a few fishing boats under patched, brown and white sails, bobbing up and down.

'Oh – !' Anna cried, jumping from her seat.

Tolcheff got up, too, and posted himself beside the window, looking as if he had especially arranged the spectacle for her.

'Look at it,' she said, 'look at that endlessness of water! A round horizon! And that colour. Good old Drasky, for getting us this far. God, it must be nice to grow up here, to live on this coast. Even when you're poor. Imagine being a child here – '

'I guess it is quite extraordinary,' Tolcheff announced.

'I've seen the Atlantic but this is different. And you know it's something no one will ever be able to spoil. You had never seen the sea, had you?'

She shook her head, sat down with her feet tucked under and stayed like that, her chin resting on her hand. 'This is perfection. A train window; the train follows the sea.'

They entered a tunnel. 'I'm sorry,' Tolcheff said.

'I don't mind. Darkness in between makes it even better.'

Now the train went in and out of tunnels for a long period. The clouds were dissolving, each re-emergence was brighter, until, after Savona, they came out under a blue sky over an intensely blue, an azure sea.

Anna put the window all the way down. The wind whipped her hair around her face and brought tears to her eyes, but she didn't want to change seats with Tolcheff, who sat across from her, riding backwards.

'Listen, next time we cross water, let's throw those two pistols away,' she asked.

'What? Why?'

She didn't answer anything, she just looked at him with a radiant face.

The train was repeatedly crossing the mouths of little rivers; when it came to the next viaduct, Tolcheff took the Webley from the seat and threw it far out. It just missed the metal crossbeams and they could see the splash it made in the stream. Anna quickly gave him the other pistol, but they were already off the viaduct.

He hesitated then, glanced slyly at her, and said, 'I want to show you something. Don't be startled.'

The train veered away from the shoreline. Between the tracks and the sea lay fields of short grass, with patches of reeds, and a few farmhouses. Tolcheff pointed the pistol at a grazing horse and fired. A very fine bang indeed, I admit.

Anna jumped, stuck her head out of the window to look back at the horse, and stared at Tolcheff.

He threw the pistol into the field. 'It's a starter pistol, for sports events. It fires blanks only.'

She seemed even more surprised than he had hoped; he

was intensely enjoying that moment. 'They wouldn't sell me a real one in Vienna, this was all I could get.' He paused. 'I meant to tell you, but then I didn't. Anyway, you wouldn't have been so impressive if you had known.'

It was the first time he had ever seen her blush.

'You must have thought very badly of me, Ann. You look ashamed now.'

She was confused. Yes, I did think badly of you, but good, too, I had built an idea on it. Which goes to show. She didn't know whether to return his happy smile or get mad. 'Oh screw,' she finally said.

He bent over and kissed her on her forehead. 'I forgive you,' he told her. 'Now you know why I didn't fire it at him.'

'At least it might have given him a nice headache.'

The train returned to the shore.

The sea wind whirling through the compartment was mixed with sudden blasts of soot from the engine, but Anna insisted on keeping the window down. The sun shone right in, and she sat with her face tilted towards it, looking out through half-closed eyes.

There were stops at little ports, stations of open platforms under tiled roofs, set in groves which were green even at that time of the year and which completely hid the houses.

Then the December sun vanished into a purple bank of clouds piling up over the sea on the southern horizon, and it was cold.

Anna closed the window, stretched out on her seat, smiled at Tolcheff, and closed her eyes. She was immediately asleep.

Tolcheff looked at himself in the little mirror under the luggage rack, framed by a photograph of Pisa and an advertisement for Strega liqueur, and rubbed a smudge of soot from his cheek with the yellow and red Draskovich handkerchief.

He was happy.

XLVI. San Remo-Cannes

He woke her up as they got near the Italian border. 'Sorry,' she muttered, yawning heartbreakingly. 'I slept like the dead. Aren't you exhausted?'

'Not yet. I don't know why not. I guess I'll suddenly keel over.'

The border station of Ventimiglia was up on the hillside. The sea, dark and secretive now, lay far below them in the rapidly falling evening. At the other side of the train, on the gaslit platform, was a great commotion of people.

They went into the corridor to look out. The third-class carriages were stormed by peasants with boxes, bales, and chickens, amidst much pushing and arguing with customs inspectors; at second class, there were families with children, and commercial travellers with big suitcases. Their first-class car remained as empty as it had been. 'It makes it easier,' Tolcheff said. 'They never bother us happy few.'

Indeed, the Italian customs inspector only nodded at them on his way through. The French official studied Anna's passport, and asked Tolcheff where he lived.

'Paris. Rue du Bac,' he said promptly.

'M'sieur, 'dame.' He touched his cap and closed the door.

'Hurrah,' Tolcheff cried. 'Welcome to France, comrade Anna. The land of brotherhood and revolution. Up to a point, anyway.'

'Whew, he made me nervous. Now I am very hungry.'

The platform cart sold them sandwiches of sausage and ham on long thin loaves of bread and a small bottle of red wine, for two lire. When he had given them their change, the man pushed his cart down a ramp and out of sight; they were his last customers, the platform had become deserted. Then there was a long unaccountable wait, with no one getting on or off, nothing moving.

Tolcheff kept leaning out of the window and sitting down: every time he looked out, a little boy in the next carriage looked out, too, and grinned at him. He frowned back, and when he looked again, a heavy lady had taken the child's place and gave him a defiant stare.

He sat down, muttering curses at the address of Draskovich. Was the stationmaster that very moment reading a wire from him, had the police started searching the train? Then the whistle blew, and when the train finally entered France, night had fallen.

All they could see now were lights from houses, villas along the coast and farms up on the hill, and at times a sudden flash of black water, hit by the revolving beam of a lighthouse.

They sat silently each in a corner, through Menton, Monaco, and Villefranche. At exactly eight fifteen, the train pulled into Nice.

They got off drunk with sleep, dazzled by the lights and the noise in the station. The next train to Cannes was not leaving until 10.00 p.m. They changed the liras they had left over, and sat in the station restaurant. There they drank cups of coffee, holding hands on the table, half dozing, feeling very close.

It was Anna who realised it was nearing ten and who got them on the local to Cannes. They arrived there at ten minutes past eleven.

Still hand in hand, they left the station and came out into a dark night in which a soft rain was falling. 'This way,' he said, pointing down the Rue de la Gare. Down to the Esplanade, those had been Draskovich's words.

It was very quiet in the streets, the gleaming pavement reflected the light of the gas lamps on the corners and from shop-windows that were electrically lit.

He smiled to himself, thinking of Draskovich's description of that sensual walk down to the sea boulevard. Here he was stumbling down those same blocks, with a half-asleep girl who let herself be dragged along, in an empty street echoing their steps.

No sensuality; tenderness.

XLVII. Cannes, Hôtel du Parc, the lobby (I)

In the lobby of the Du Parc, Anna let herself be installed in an easy chair, screened by palms growing out of huge stone pots. Tolcheff went to ask for Draskovich.

'Mr Draskovich hasn't arrived, he cabled a delay.'

'Ah. And Counsellor Zidkin?'

The receptionist studied the register. 'Secretary Zidkin? Third Secretary Zidkin from Paris?'

'Yes, yes, of course.' Where the hell did I get my idea that he was a counsellor? That's a high rank. How stupid of me, my telegrams were addressed wrong then.

'Mr Zidkin arrived yesterday, and he is now staying in the Draskovich suite.'

'I'll see him, please. I am Constantin Grunwald, of the Russian Embassy in Vienna. It's urgent.'

The receptionist shook his head, studied the keys behind him, and said, 'He is not in yet, Mr Grunwald. I came on at four this afternoon, and I have not seen the gentleman.'

'I'll wait.' He took a chair next to Anna and turned it towards the entrance. It was nearly midnight. The lobby was empty just then, and Anna was sleeping, huddled up like a child.

Chances are that Draskovich didn't wire him or anything. He doesn't bother about his underlings. Maybe, maybe he wants his people to worry, and then he'll arrive on the scene as a tough man who escaped from a kidnap outrage. That way, those wires he thinks we sent wouldn't make him look stupid. Yes, that is likely. Suppose the receptionist had said, Mr Draskovich is upstairs. But I knew he wasn't. I think I've got a pretty good insight now into the way his mind works.

Let's consider this Zidkin. I can conjure up two very different types coming in through that revolving door. Zidkin A, an old man, but hefty, completely bald, a criminal type, carrying a cane with a hidden sword blade, a bully. Zidkin B, a junior Draskovich, very smart and diplomaty, drinking Scotches and calling the waiter 'fellow'. A vicarious bully, like his boss. Either would be the kind of assistant Draskovich could use. I don't know which one will be better for our plans. Neither seems to fit in with them somehow, when you look close.

Tolcheff was wide awake, because he was very worried. His plans, and reality until then, had had little in common.

The real Zidkin entered the hotel at half past twelve and in the highest of spirits. A day in which he had made himself thoroughly at home, had bought a French pullover, beach shoes, and cologne in shops on the Croisette, had won some more money, and had made the acquaintance of a charming woman. She had commented on the book he'd been reading on a café terrace in the warm sun, she had been surprised when he told her he wasn't French, and tomorrow she was coming to have lunch with him in the hotel. His address did wonders everywhere; shop clerks wrote it down with a special expression on their faces. He hadn't said anything to her about police work.

Zidkin was singing to himself his favourite song of that day, 'Je cherche fortune, autour du Chat Noir, au clair de la lune . . . ,' but the moment he emerged from the revolving door and saw Tolcheff look at him from between two palm trees, he stopped and his heart sank.

Some intuition told him that that man was sitting there waiting for him, was connected with Draskovich, and had come to end the marvellous time he was having.

The receptionist caught Tolcheff's eye and nodded. Tolcheff stood up. For one wild second, Zidkin considered turning around and escaping, but instead he walked up and said, 'Zidkin. Are you waiting for me?'

Tolcheff pumped his hand. 'I am Constantin Grunwald, attaché at our embassy in Vienna. I sent you a wire about my arrival.'

Zidkin threw a vague look towards the mail rack. It wouldn't do perhaps to say he had been out all day. He sat down.

Tolcheff remained standing. He felt certain of a sudden that it was all going to work. All's well that ends well. The irony in Draskovich's voice when he had mentioned Zidkin. The youngish face, but a bit pathetic with the hair precisely arranged over the thin spot. A new cashmere pullover, bright burgundy, sitting in a dark grey, almost black, office-type suit, shiny, too. Two French novels, several newspapers, in the left hand.

Tolcheff took the drafts of the telegrams for Marseilles and Petersburg, which Draskovich had written on the train, out of his pocket. 'Perhaps we'd better go up to the suite,' he said.

Zidkin had been afraid he'd say that. It was the last thing he wanted to do; it pained him the way Tolcheff referred to it as 'the' suite. He didn't want it to become common ground, it was still his.

'It's quiet here,' he said, 'and room service is terribly slow at this time. You must want a drink. What would you like?'

'Just coffee then,' Tolcheff said, sitting down, too.

'And who is the pretty young lady with you?' Zidkin asked, looking at Anna, asleep with her head against the back of the chair.

'Oh, she is – she is Anna.'

'I see,' Zidkin said, afraid to ask more. He began to feel increasingly that his week in Cannes was doomed.

XLVIII. Cannes, Hôtel du Parc, the lobby (II)

'You got his telegram. Undersecretary Draskovich is staying in Milan for a while,' Tolcheff said, putting as much innuendo in those few words as he could. 'He sent me on to Cannes.'

Zidkin, sombrely stirring his coffee, didn't look up. 'Why does he address me as "counsellor"?' he asked.

'Why? Eh – well, you know Draskovich.'

It seemed a satisfactory explanation; Zidkin nodded. He was on the point of asking about the '3S', but thought the better of it.

'This letter here,' Tolcheff said, 'he wants to be delivered to the court in Marseilles tomorrow. "Tell him to take it there himself," he said. This one, for Petersburg, has to be cabled through Paris, in the regular diplomatic code. We didn't have the book with us.'

'Did you join him in Vienna, Mr Grunwald?'

All he has to do is look up the diplomatic list and he'll see there is no Grunwald. 'Yes, he decided he needed another assistant. He said – but never mind that.'

'He said what?'

'Never mind. Don't worry. He's too damn hard on people.'

If Tolcheff had known Zidkin's thoughts, he wouldn't have bothered with these psychological manœuvres. Zidkin was preoccupied, but not with the identity of Tolcheff-Grunwald.

'Then there's the press conference,' Tolcheff went on.

'What? A press conference about what?'

'Well, read the letters, Zidkin,' Tolcheff said, already

assuming the tone Zidkin was usually addressed in.

These, too, failed to arouse Zidkin's interest or suspicion. 'I see he's changed his mind again,' was his only comment.

Tolcheff was surprised at his own clearheadedness. His thoughts flew, it all seemed to fall into place. 'Press conference on Monday, for the major local journalists. In Marseilles, in the office of our commercial attaché. Draskovich said, "If we do this, we may as well do it properly, not furtively. Get credit for it." You see his point.'

'Why on Monday? Why so soon?'

'Because – well, in time for Christmas, of course. The spirit of forgiveness.'

'But why is he coming to France, then?' With that question, Zidkin seemed to rally himself.

Why indeed. 'Well, you know Draskovich,' Tolcheff replied, and again it seemed a satisfactory answer.

'You don't have to do it,' Tolcheff went on, trying not to smile at his own ingenuity. 'I mean, the press conference. Drasky said in fact, if you don't feel up to it, we should wait for him. It needs faultless French, he said, plus a feel for French journalism.'

'It so happens I think I have both.'

'Do you? Well, fine then. I'll sit beside you and help with coffees and paper and all that.'

'You call him Drasky?' Zidkin, whose thoughts seemed to wander again, now asked.

'He was an old friend of my father's.'

'I wouldn't have guessed he ever was a friend of anybody's.' Just then, Zidkin's innate prudence had evaporated.

'Come on now, Zidkin. Don't hold it against the man that he changes his decision. He must have – '

'Oh screw his decision,' Zidkin interrupted, surprising himself and throwing a guilty look at Anna. 'That's not it. I have engagements here. Eh, connected with my own work in Paris. You see, for the first time . . . And now here's Draskovich again with his damned orders. Drasky!' He checked himself.

'Well, but I'll be happy to help you. I can take that letter to Marseilles tomorrow, for instance. Just get me an official envelope. And I can wire to the newspapers for you. Anything you say. I've nothing to do here but wait for Draskovich's arrival.'

These words instilled new life in Zidkin. 'That would be very kind of you,' he said. Then, for the first time suspiciously, he asked, 'Where are we to get the funds for this?'

'Draskovich gave a cheque to draw on. Here.'

Zidkin looked and whistled. 'Five thousand francs. Well. With me he used to quibble over every penny.'

Tolcheff shrugged modestly. 'It has to be countersigned by the Ambassador. You'll have it back on Friday or Saturday. I guess we can charge things if need be, with the hotel here.'

'Where are you staying in Cannes?' Zidkin asked conversationally. He now felt the worst had been averted, and took a sip of his coffee.

'I haven't taken a room yet. We came in only just now, so I thought, I'd see you first, and install Anna here.'

Zidkin put his cup back down on the saucer. 'Here? Why is that?'

'She's Draskovich's girl friend. One of them, I guess. He didn't want her around in Milan, so I escorted her to Cannes for him. She is to stay in his suite and wait for him.'

'What!' Zidkin cried. He jumped up, knocking his knee against the table and spilling his coffee, and his cry turned every face in the lobby towards them. Even Anna opened her eyes and then closed them again.

'What's the matter with you?' Tolcheff asked.

Zidkin sat down and bent his head towards him; he looked as if he were about to burst into tears. 'Listen, Grunwald,' he whispered, 'please help. I'm in that suite and I need it. Tomorrow, oh well, you understand . . . I didn't ask for this. I didn't expect it. But then that wire came, a whole week, and it seemed as if for the first time in my life . . . and now . . . Please put her somewhere else. Just till Draskovich arrives. The Gonnet et de la Reine, for instance, right near here, much more intimate and cosy, really. Less, well, you know.'

Tolcheff hesitated. 'But you see, we had to leave in such a hurry. She has no luggage. And I only have that government cheque. I don't see myself arrive in the middle of the night at a place where they don't know Draskovich, and have them put up a girl all by herself. She won't like that either.'

'Here, allow me,' Zidkin said urgently. 'Fifty, a hundred francs. I'll come with you, I'll help. I was there only this afternoon for tea, they were terribly polite. You should stay there, too. An excellent place. No, please take it.'

'All right then. In that case, I'll leave the cheque with you. You handle the money. It's made out to bearer.'

'I'm really grateful,' Zidkin assured him, already taking a step towards the door. Tolcheff shook Anna gently and hoisted her up, and they followed him, she with her eyes closed.

XLIX. Cannes, and Dvinsk

A brilliant, almost blue light came in between the curtains, which hadn't been pulled quite closed, and filled the room. Anna searched for her watch on the night table beside the bed and couldn't find it. But there was a piece of paper, a note from Tolcheff: 'I'll be back by evening. My room is two doors down, 524. Have a nice day. Avoid Zidkin, like the plague.' There was also a small pile of French money.

She stretched, it felt marvellous to lie in that narrow, neat bed. She didn't remember anything after the Cannes station. I had really had it. I'm naked, Tolcheff must have undressed me. A pleasant idea for some reason. I wonder if it worked, those telegram drafts he was going to present as letters to

Zidkin. I wish I could remember how this Zidkin looked, I must have seen him last night. And how did Andrew get us in this hotel.

She got up and looked around the room first. He had put her dress on a hanger and her underwear was in the basin, which was filled with soapy water. She fished it out and wrung it. What a, a friendly thing to do. He must be used to washing out his own things every evening, wherever he is. A life alone.

She read the 'Notice to Travellers', and saw on a card in the wardrobe that the room was for one person only, and cost four francs fifty with breakfast. Then she opened the curtains.

Her room was high up in the hotel, under the eaves, which she could see on each side. But it faced south, over the Croisette, and over the sea, which lay before her even more radiant than when she had first seen it the day before. A light breeze made the water and the flags along the boulevard ripple, and the sky and the sea reflected each other's blueness. The sun is high, it must be near noon. She remembered that her watch was in Genoa. She draped herself in a blanket and opened the window.

It didn't feel as good as she had thought. It's all unfair. With what right am I here, and that man with his panama, and that woman with her silver foxes? Who is busy getting the food together they will eat tonight?

Oh come on girl. Let's have no Tolcheffisms. But I do understand Sophia better. I wouldn't have wanted to shoot that Judge in some dark office in Petersburg, but his presence here, after what he did, was offensive. An offence against God or nature. You have to be innocent, or at the least without judgement on others, to be allowed this indulgence.

Later, as she walked through the town, those thoughts condensed into a vague feeling of being in a garden. Like the birdhouse in the zoo. Cold outside; behind the glass, warmth and all colours. The Garden of Eden was God's zoo. No thoughts. Peace, pleasure.

She had nothing on under her dress, because the underwear hadn't dried. She liked the sensation of her thighs touching each other, and of the material of her dress rubbing her breasts.

But as she was sitting in a tearoom, gazing out on to the sunny street, and without thinking about what she was doing, eating the sugar out of her empty teacup, squeezing a drop of lemon on each spoonful, she heard a voice. She turned her head and saw a tall, oldish man in a cream-coloured suit and with a soft straw hat he held in his hand. He had a yachtsman's wrinkled tan and with the self-assured smile of the rich he was saying something to her. She didn't hear what, because – she didn't quite understand why – she got so angry that there was a buzzing in her ears. She swallowed; the man moved a chair back as if to sit down at her table; she thought she saw a kind of smirk on his face, the glazed look of a dog. . . . 'You want to make love to me, is that it?' she said quite loudly. 'You want to hire my body to put your old thin legs against? Don't you think there's already a smell of death about you? Shouldn't you – ?' But at that point the man had put his straw hat back on and fled the tearoom.

She was sure people were staring at her; she didn't look up. Her anger had vanished; she wasn't upset at what she had done, she smiled at herself. Poor devil, why shouldn't he make a pass at a girl? What's so precious about my belly? It's not his fault that things are arranged that way. But that's not what made me so mad, it wasn't outraged virtue, but, but what? Outraged humanity? I mean, humanness? She didn't quite understand herself, but that word was precise. I hope I'm not letting Tolcheff fanaticise me. No, I'm not, not in the least. But it did seem an outrage that that old man in his straw hat made life so easy for himself, too easy, while Tolcheff makes his so bitterly difficult.

Oh dammit, Anna, watch it, or you'll be nowhere at home except in your school. You don't want to rebel and you don't quietly enjoy the good things of life. The good things – what a repulsive expression.

Oh, she answered herself, it's just that I hate weakness, indulgence.

She put the money down for her tea and walked out. She followed the Rue d'Antibes, crossed a covered market where an orgy of fish and lobsters and oysters had been brought in, and poinsettia and holly for Christmas, and then round herself back at the railroad station.

She went in and stood for a while on a platform, watching a train for Paris leave. She read the time schedules on the wall, repeating the names to herself, Marseilles, Biarritz, Madrid, London, and those of her own train, which were printed in red, the express going back east, Milan, Vienna, Warsaw, Dvinsk, Petersburg. That same instant, that one second she singled out by biting her lip and feeling the pain, Dvinsk existed. Its dark, dirty, snowy roads leading to an empty railroad quay with its ice-cold wind, damp bread sticking to the newspaper wrapping, putting on shoes over socks full of holes, coughing under a blanket weighted down with your overcoat, your body your enemy.

But right here, behind those windows on the top floor of the Rue d'Antibes, windows she had looked up at because they were reflecting the low sun as if made of crystal or diamond, people were dying, too, or crying with despair. Dvinsk was better then, perhaps, more true to the human fate. Easier to be mortal in Dvinsk.

As she passed the luggage office, she pulled out her passport, Tolcheff's sister's passport, and told the man behind the counter that she had forgotten a little suitcase on the Petersburg Express of the day before. A few minutes later he brought it to her.

She ate and went back to the hotel. Now she could have put on clean things, but she didn't bother. She put the suitcase down and stayed as she was. She sat in the window sill, staring out over the sea.

Late in the afternoon, with darkness falling, she became restless. She put a note on Tolcheff's door, to make sure he'd know she was waiting. Not only that I am not meant for his kind of place, she thought, but the only people who look right here are those fishermen on the quay, with their bare feet, and their piles of fish gut the tourists go around in a big detour. They fit. Sunshine and poverty. All that money doesn't belong here, it is greasy, and this is a poor, dry country; it's money from the cold northern cities, you can tell. You don't need theories, just a sense of smell.

There was a knock and Tolcheff came in. He stood still, trying to adjust to the twilight. Anna jumped up and turned on the lamp. 'Oh I'm glad to see you,' she said, 'I was getting melancholic.'

'With this?' He pointed to the sea, the gaily lit boulevard, the lighthouse, and the sparkling row of lights along the promontory to the west, where there was still a touch of red in the air after the sunset. Voices, carriages, softly in the dusk.

'Do you like it here, Andrew?'

'Well, yes. . . . It was quite a day, but it all went damn well. I was on the eight thirty to Marseilles, and I got to the court registrar just as he was about to vanish for the day, and I handed him the Draskovich text about cancelling all proceedings, and he didn't raise an eyebrow, he seemed pleased.'

'Didn't it look very odd and unofficial, on that sheet of paper?'

'Oh no. I had been to Zidkin before leaving. He wasn't happy at all to see me, he said he needed his rest and was getting ill from the lack of sleep Draskovich was causing him. But he wanted to get rid of me, that's what counted. He sealed the letter in an embassy cover. He wrote the invitation for the press conference, and the hotel is wiring it for him to the proper papers. When I closed his door, he was getting back into bed. Press conference on Monday. That was the earliest possible.'

'Monday . . . And if Draskovich shows up before?'

'He won't. I'm inside that man's head. He won't, he'll lie low for a week. Or even till after Christmas, I bet you.'

'How is Zidkin?' she asked. 'Sort of nice then?'

'God, no, he's just a bit of an idiot, I think. Nothing nice

out him, he joined the secret police once, so in the end he
must be a brute like the rest of them. But I'm beginning to
see that those people all hate each other, too, not just us...
Or anyway, they have no illusions about each other, they
take it for granted they're all frauds or crooks.'

'Then what? Did you see Sophia?'

'I saw the prison. I walked past it. Pretty awful on a day
like this, those rows of tiny black windows in a high wall
and then this sun shining on it. I couldn't very well go in to
see her, not yet, we have to finish this first. I'm Constantin
Grunwald at the moment, of the Vienna embassy.'

She laughed nervously. 'And without anyone asking for
your papers?'

'Well, no, we're all gentlemen, you see, trusting each
other.'

'I'm not sure I understand. If they take it for granted of
each other they're all crooks . . . ?'

'Yes, Ann, but gentlemen-crooks. Like in real life. Zidkin
doesn't know what to make of me, because I act nicely with
him, and he can't see what I get out of it. They wouldn't do
that. But they wouldn't question one's word about who you
are either. It's crookedness on another level. The rules of
some kind of game are observed, mostly, I think.'

'Oh . . . But you don't mind asking them favours, even
this Zidkin, idiot or not? You don't mind joining their
shabby games?'

'Mind?' He shrugged vehemently. 'Mind? Who cares?
They've all got blood on their hands, for God's sake, don't
lose sight of that, anything goes for them. So let's be
Machiavellian. They're our sworn enemies, all those little
gentlemen. Everyone. They did the swearing. For that
matter, those ladies and gentlemen out there on the boulevard, too. It's true. There isn't enough to go around on
earth, there isn't enough for all this,' and he waved his hand
to take in the hotel, the sea, the Croisette, the lights. 'Melo-
dramatic?' he asked. 'No, dramatic. True.'

'But you said before, how you liked it here, and you
wanted me to admire the view.'

He answered, 'Because the people . . ' She closed her eye
just for one moment, but he had seen it, and stopped talking

She didn't ask what he meant. She looked at the sea, black
with a line of moving white where the foam reflected the
boulevard lights; she tried to distinguish the sound of those
waves breaking. Her secret just then was, not that she was
tired of listening to his ideas, but her feeling of pity for him
which had come back.

After a long silence she said, 'You look nice.'

'I bought a new shirt. I had to, I smelled.'

'I got my suitcase. Not that there's much in it. I'm going
to throw away those damn pumps, though. Can I?'

'Yes, please do.'

'Do you want to make love?' she asked, pulling off her
dress over her head. She heard the intake of his breath when
he saw she was nude underneath. That pleased her,
changed her mood to excitement. She walked over to her bed
and lay down.

As he leaned over her, she held him back with her hand
against his shoulders and said, 'Promise now, not to be so
hasty.'

She told him, 'I made several discoveries today.'

'Name 'em.'

'One. I'd rather live in Dvinsk than in Cannes.'

'What?'

'Two. I'd rather die in Dvinsk than in Cannes.'

'Hmm.'

'Three, you're not specially selfless. It's that you are
another species. You want to be just, like someone else
wants to be rich.'

'Another species. Higher on the scale of evolution?'

She considered that. 'Yes, maybe. Perhaps that's why
you're not as tough as we are. Just as we must seem less
tough to a bulldog or a ferret.'

'Oh.' She could hear he didn't like that very much.

'It's good. It doesn't make you weak, it means you're on
the side of life. I don't mean pseudo-Darwin survival stuff
Life, living. All those creatures hanging on, you know, oh

en, thin babies – that's why I like you now.' And she put
er hand on him.

'And why we made love?' he asked.

'Maybe.'

'Oh well . . . any reason will do in a pinch.'

L. Cannes, Hôtel du Parc, the Draskovich suite (I)

n the morning of the press conference, Tolcheff-Grunwald
ound Zidkin on the balcony of the Du Parc suite, staring at
tray with breakfast put in front of him.

It was very early; it was just getting light over the sea.
ut it wasn't cold, though Zidkin, fully dressed, sat with a
lanket around him.

'Sea air, to brace the nerves,' was the first thing he said.
'm not nervous because of the press conference, mind you.
m nervous because it is too early, and because of Drasko-
ich. They just brought this up.' He handed Tolcheff a
legram.

It was addressed to Third Secretary Zidkin ('At least he's
ropped that counsellor joke') and read, 'Am arriving
Monday 24 December at 2 p.m. Meet me at the Cannes
ation. Was delayed through bodily duress and further
elayed through the inefficiency of Italian tailors. Notify
rench border police and apologise for 19 December.
onvene local press for Friday 28 December. No slip-ups
lease. Also order Agua de Vetiver green Birkenwasser
nd Cachets de Fèvre. Draskovich 3S.'

'Hmm,' Tolcheff said. 'An interesting telegram.'

'I admit, Grunwald, that I am heartily sick of your
rasky. What is all this? And do you know what? The cheque
me back from Paris yesterday, the Ambassador refused to

countersign it. No explanation. And I had ordered a cold buffet and wine for twenty from one of the best places in Marseilles.'

'You had? Why?'

'It's the custom,' Zidkin announced, 'in France, when you invite the press.

'He'll pay you back. He's an undersecretary, after all. He'd want you to do it properly.'

'But he tells us to postpone it . . . ! But you know what?'

'What?'

'I've already sent off a report to our Ambassador. I have that right. One, that Draskovich made an unauthorised break in his official journey and that he is messing around shopping and whoring. (I didn't put it that way, of course.) Two, he gave us a cheque that's no good. Three, he uses the diplomatic wires, expensive as they are, for private jokes and insults. Like this telegram here. Do you realise it has seventy-three words including the stops? He could have said what he has to say in ten. You know how much that would have saved, in roubles or in francs? And do you think he can send a fellow diplomat out to buy his Birkenwasser, whatever the hell that is?'

'It's for your hair,' Tolcheff said with a smile.

'In the police, everyone has the right to check up on everyone,' Zidkin said with sudden complacency. 'I have every right to check on your Drasky and report directly to the Ambassador. I think the Ambassador doesn't like him at all. He calls him an upstart.'

'Oh, well and good. He's not my Drasky, though. But what do you think all this means, about tailoring, and duress, and apologising for 19 December? And what is 3S?' Tolcheff asked ingenuously.

Zidkin shrugged so angrily that he lost his blanket. 'I haven't the foggiest notion. Bodily duress. I think it's another allusion to his sexual adventures in Milan. He's used that "3S" before, I was going to ask you. I figure it means that he has three girls, Draskovich of the three signorinas, in Italian, you see. Between you and me, the man revolts me.

e once made me come with him to a brothel, in Paris, and
ter he'd had himself a bottle of champagne, he told that as
student he was called Draskovich with the three pricks. So
guess we're still on that. And the bodily duress means he's
crewing himself into the ground.' This sudden vulgarity
ade Zidkin himself blush. 'Françoise agrees that men who
o on so, actually don't have much to . . .'

Tolcheff said, 'I wondered about that "3S", I thought it
as a kind of police code.'

'What would that be for? As you can see, Draskovich likes
advertise all his moves, those on the ground and those in
ed.'

'Well, it takes all sorts, he's a show-off. A pity though, for
l the work we did for today. You would have done well.
wonder if we can still reach everyone and postpone the
vitations.'

'Dammit, Grunwald, it will be terribly embarrassing. And
cançoise had finally promised to come and hear me speak.'

The main reason for Zidkin's new detachment from the
rvice and rebellion against Undersecretary Draskovich was
e large number of waking hours he had spent in his Du
arc bed with this Françoise. She was the girl whose atten-
on he had attracted his first day, by sitting on a café terrace
ith the novel *A Rebours*. It had created a turnabout in his
ind and body, though it was too early to tell if the change
ould be lasting.

'Françoise is my lady friend,' he added. 'She is a local girl,
real lady, she works in an art gallery. She thinks I should
it and live in France, and be an artist perhaps.'

'I know what,' Tolcheff said. 'Let's stick to our plans and
nore this. You just go ahead and go to Marseilles and do
e press conference. And let me stay here and meet Drasky
the station. I'll explain to him that his wire came after
u'd left. You just forget about this.' And he crumpled the
legram into a ball and tossed it over the balcony.

Zidkin broke a croissant into crumbs. 'But he'll ask why
u didn't send a telegram to Marseilles to stop me,' he
ggested.

'I'll say, "With the invitations out, I had thought you'd
prefer to go on." Anyway, he'll be here at two, you start in
Marseilles at three. If he insists, we'll wire you immediately.'

'You're right.' Zidkin stood up. 'I'm off. But you will
wire me, if he's really livid.'

'Absolutely. Will you be back tonight?'

'At nine o'clock. She and I were going back together on
the evening express train.'

'Perhaps I'll meet you at the station and we'll exchange
notes. You're doing me a favour, too. I don't want to hang
around for a press conference on Friday. Do you have the
statement?'

'Yes.' Zidkin now started to observe the amenities. 'How
is your hotel, and how is Miss Anna?'

'Fine, fine.'

'Help yourself to coffee and everything.'

'You better run, Zidkin.'

When he had gone, Tolcheff emptied Zidkin's cup in the
flower box and poured himself new coffee with milk which
was still hot. Christ, that was a struggle. And a very narrow
escape, folks. If we hadn't distributed his suits among the
rural population, he'd have shown up on Saturday. .
What weird luck. But if Ann and I had done what we theor-
ised about so, killed him and sent off the message that he had
defected, then Sophia would have been really safe, with none
of these risks that it'll all suddenly unravel and collapse. And
none of these messy tricks. The simplicity of violence. The
simplicity of power, Draskovich would say.

But that's chaotic, no what is the word, syncretic, to sit
here and drink coffee and watch the sun rise over the Mediterranean, and deliberate, all by yourself, without appeal to
a god or your fellow men and women, to the party, or even
to one friend, whether you have the right to kill someone.
That is what's wrong. If I pretend to that, we all can, everyone everywhere, and there is no line of history left, no road
to revolution, only a thousand little adventures and murders,
the world turned into a thousand little medieval Italian
princedoms with poison rings and daggers. It's not meant to

happen like that.

The simplicity of power: like a wide, marble staircase leading up to a kind of throne, and on its steps men fighting each other to death? No, that looks more like an opera. The reality is deadly, but grey.

The sun was well above the horizon now. He poured more coffee and started to stuff his pockets with croissants.

Then the door flew open, and Zidkin dashed back into the room.

'Now what?' Tolcheff cried, dropping a roll.

'I forgot,' Zidkin panted, 'that I have to clear out of here. It's his suite. The swine. He just couldn't let me have my week.'

He began to throw things into his suitcase.

'I'll do it. I'll take your stuff to the Gonnet,' Tolcheff said.

'And you'll put the girl in here?'

'Just go! Just don't miss your train.'

LI. Cannes, the railroad station (I)

Then he discovered the solution, not in spite but because of its absurdity.

At two in the afternoon, on the arrival platform of the Cannes railroad station, he would indeed be there and await Draskovich. No trick played on Zidkin; there had simply been no reason to tell Zidkin who it was that would meet Draskovich there. No tricks, the truth.

It was a hesitant day. The springlike clearness was slowly dimming, the sky was opaque but the sun was still visible. You still felt you were in the south, there was no darkness in nature, although Christmas, the Western Christmas of the Gregorian calendar, was but a day away. To Tolcheff, the decorations, the holly and red flowers and wreaths, seemed very odd in the soft light of the Mediterranean.

The nostalgia of lamplight on dark afternoons, snowflakes outside the window, that was his association with December childhood. But it was a vague one, thought up afterwards perhaps, from books. His own childhood had been too haphazard, too confused, to have had any real images like that. And so he was happy in Cannes with the absence of them, with the strangeness of a year ending in soft wind, blue and grey gentle seas, occasional half-sunshine warm enough for people to read their papers at the little tables of sidewalk cafés.

He wasn't particularly nervous but he had no idea what he was going to say. The only concrete point was, to make sure Draskovich wouldn't forestall the three o'clock Marseilles press conference, which would put the seal on Sophia's safety. Not mentioning it would be enough to achieve that.

Why am I going at all then?

Simple: to show I'm not one of them.

The train came in punctually; it was crowded because of the holiday week that had begun. Even the first-class carriages let out a stream of passengers. The platform was already emptying when he saw Draskovich get off, accompanied by a porter carrying all those same suitcases. Tolcheff laughed aloud, there was something idiotic about it. I guess they're all full again, with the same kind of stuff, except he couldn't find Birkenwasser in Genoa. Then he saw at Draskovich's side a wiry, dark man with a moustache, keeping in step with him. A French policeman, no doubt. It was true then, he did have himself met at the border.

He saw Draskovich look up and down the platform for Zidkin, then start walking towards the exit. The policeman was talking and Draskovich was listening with an attentive little smile. Then Draskovich saw him.

Tolcheff had posted himself near the exit gate, on the platform side of the control booth. Draskovich stood still and they looked at each other. The policeman took a few more steps, and then he, too, stopped, uncertainly.

They were still twenty or thirty feet apart but Tolcheff saw Draskovich's face with unnatural clarity, the smooth skin (he must have had himself a nice rest in Genoa), the large ears (Tolcheff now realised for the first time), and those strange eyes, a bit watery, glaucous, and yet sharp and intense. They're what frightened Ann that first time. Eyes that have seen everything and seen it without surprise and without pity.

He hesitates. He wonders if I've come to assassinate him after all.

He looks different. He has all new clothes on, that's why. Very sharp, too; he looks like an Italian confidence man.

That discovery made Tolcheff grin, and it was probably the grin that decided Draskovich. He walked on without saying anything to his French escort, and it seemed as if he were going to walk right past. Tolcheff took a step forward and said firmly in French, 'Undersecretary Draskovich? I'm Grunwald, attaché of embassy, here to greet you. Secretary Zidkin is unfortunately not in Cannes.'

Draskovich's split second of blankness. When he decides to lie, or beat a retreat, or pull a fast one, as he calls it.

'How do you do, Grunwald. This is police detective Labrunie. Attaché Grunwald.'

Handshakes.

'So Zidkin absented himself, did he? You see, Labrunie, a good thing I wired your chief myself. Young men left alone on that Côte d'Azur of yours . . .'

The French policeman laughed rather long.

'Your suite is waiting for you at the Du Parc Hôtel, Mr Undersecretary,' Tolcheff said. 'Perhaps you'd like to go on foot? It's only a few blocks, and it is a very pleasant walk.

'Yes, I'm acquainted with it,' Draskovich said. 'But I think it would be better to drive. Perhaps you would be good enough to get me a cab.'

'Allow me,' the officer suggested.

'No, no, dear colleague. Grunwald doesn't mind, he has young legs.'

Tolcheff went out to hail a cab, and he seated himself in it, on one of the folding seats facing backward. Draskovich didn't comment on it, and the three of them drove to the hotel.

'I'll leave you here then, Mr Undersecretary,' the officer said. 'When would you like me to come back?'

'Oh no, I insist you come up for a drink,' Draskovich said. 'Grunwald and I have no secrets.'

LII. Cannes, Hôtel du Parc, the Draskovich suite (II)

Draskovich ignored Tolcheff's presence as he went around the suite, had the balcony doors opened, luggage taken to his bedroom, tea served for himself and an apéritif for the French policeman. Tolcheff went out on the balcony. He saw that he had dropped Zidkin's coffee spoon in the flower box that morning and poked around in the earth with it. The sky was darkening now, and he shivered and went back inside. Through the open door he saw Draskovich in his bedroom, taking things out of his dispatch case. The Frenchman was sipping at his glass, looking puzzled. Tolcheff entered the bedroom.

'You owe me at least four thousand francs, for things missing, presumed stolen,' Draskovich said without turning around.

'That still leaves a thousand out of the five thousand you owe me. You were going to let me taste life as it's really lived. I couldn't get your cheque cashed.'

'Is that why you are here? What have you done with Zidkin?'

'But we did strike a bargain,' Tolcheff said lightly. 'And

you weren't going to retract those telegrams.'

Draskovich looked at him for a moment. 'You don't amuse me. This is the last time I'll ever let you speak to me. Make the most of it if you have something to say. There was no bargain, for you didn't release me. Your idiot friends in Genoa did.' He laughed his little laugh and turned around. In the mirror he could see the French policeman, who was pouring himself another drink from the carafe. 'You people really give me a pain in the ass. Your friends don't even stick by you. What on earth do you think you'll ever achieve, you're all so fucking noble. We do better for our friends, I assure you.'

He had used those same words speaking to Anna once.

'Ah,' Tolcheff answered, lifting a finger, 'but you people don't seem to have any friends. You, Zidkin, the Ambassador, you're all such backbiters. I never knew before how our betters all hate each other so. I wonder why, isn't there enough to go around, even for you happy few?'

'Where's Zidkin?' Draskovich asked again. Tolcheff looked at his watch and did not answer.

'There's a warrant out for your arrest in Italy,' Draskovich told him. 'Simple theft, but I hear they have pretty stiff sentences there. It's also being reported to the headquarters in Brussels, so maybe it will be turned into an international warrant. That should really crown your career.' He scrutinised Tolcheff, who had turned pale. 'What, did you think old Draskovich wouldn't mind losing all his things?'

'What do you mean, the headquarters in Brussels?' But this is crazy. Draskovich reporting me to the secretariat of the Second International? Does he know about me?

'The train company headquarters,' Draskovich said impatiently. 'The Compagnie Internationale des Wagons-lits.'

'Oh – oh!' Tolcheff smiled broadly. Then he said, 'Zidkin has just completed a press conference for you. He announced that you'll abide by the results of the French justice and that there'll be no further action, that the case Derkheim is closed. And then he added something about Christmas and forgiveness.'

If Draskovich was shocked or angry, he didn't show it. 'How did you put him up to that? With those idiotic telegrams from Milan?'

'In a way. A bit more complicated than that. I understand there's to be a nice cold buffet afterwards, for twenty. He'll bring you the bill.'

Draskovich sat down on a bed. 'Be with you in a moment, Labrunie,' he called, 'don't go away. I may need you, ha ha.' Then, softly, 'Zidkin is a stupid goddamn fool. This'll give me a most welcome opportunity to get rid of him. You're actually saving me all kinds of trouble, Tolcheff. You don't understand anything. If you and that girl of yours hadn't shown up, I'd probably have decided to drop the case anyway. I was just about ready to forget Derkheim, period.'

'Well, then, we're all satisfied. And don't be too hard on Zidkin. You know, he's reporting on you, irregularities in your travels, cheques that bounce, sexual extravaganzas . . .'

'Sexual extravaganzas?'

'I didn't know you people had the right to inform on each other, without regard to rank. Very democratic. Or more like a colony of rats. Though perhaps that is unfair to rats.'

Draskovich only got offended when he chose to. 'Tell me about the extravaganzas Zidkin reported,' he said.

'Well, there was that 3S business. What does it mean? You can tell me now.'

'It's the code for official police telegrams, what else? I figured your Anna might know somehow, through her father. I didn't want a bullet in my stomach from that hysterical female.'

'Really? On the level?'

'Yes, yes, damn you.'

'Well, Zidkin never heard of it. After careful deduction, he decided it meant you were bedding three signorinas in Milan.'

'I will keep him,' Draskovich said almost dreamily. 'A man like that is valuable. I will keep him for the next occasion when we need an unidentified corpse floating down the Seine.'

'Poor Zidkin. I don't think you're joking.'

'Oh, but I assure you I'm not, Andy the Fix. You and I follow different rules. And once more, that's why you will never make it. There's something about you, I admit that. You should have grabbed that chance I offered you to get out. I don't say it was on the level, who knows. You will never know. But you'll never get another one. You're with the losers now, for keeps. You're all the same, you – what do you call yourself? Reds?'

'No, not precisely.'

'You're like bugs crawling under the feet of society, you think it's a victory when you make us scratch. You think you're too noble and fine to put your hands on the levers of power, at best you try to blow up some poor president or some senile haemophiliac king. But that's not where power lies. Either a man wants something or he doesn't. You are simply too soft and too weak. If you were a real man . . .'

'But you see, us Reds, we're not interested in real men. We're interested in men. In mankind. In the people.'

Draskovich shrugged. 'I flattered you. You are a peasant. So go on being one. You make me sick with your it – isn't – fair crap. Do worms tell crows it isn't fair? They at least have the decency to shut up while they're eaten. So be a worm,' with a smile that he seemed to expect Tolcheff would share. 'And now, get out.'

'I once told myself I should have held out my hand to you, and invited you to join the brotherhood of man.'

'Oh, Christ. It's only you people who want to crawl in each other's laps all the time. Because you're weak, weak. I said, fuck off.'

'Don't be rude,' Tolcheff answered.

Draskovich had got up, and Tolcheff was now standing in the other room. The old game of the policeman: through some reflex, Draskovich decided at that very moment to switch from what he considered urbanity to the Draskovich who inspired fear. Though Tolcheff was already leaving, Draskovich's face went dead, his soft hands opened and closed. He came out of his bedroom after Tolcheff. 'I said, fuck off. Go fuck that friend of yours. Or no. Go tell her about the Cause. Girls like that come with their heads instead of their cunts.'

Tolcheff took a step back from the door towards the table.

'You're so soft,' Draskovich said, 'that it'll be a pleasure stepping on you. There won't – '

What interrupted his words was the very hot tea water served by the Hôtel du Parc; Tolcheff had picked the teapot off the table and thrown the contents in his face.

Draskovich gave a scream. Knocking over glasses and the sugar bowl, he grabbed a napkin and pressed it against his eyes. The French policeman jumped up and looked from one to the other, his hand inside his jacket. Tolcheff looked at this scene with as much surprise as if he had played no role in it. He went into the bathroom and came out with a towel dipped in cold water.

Draskovich didn't accept it. He walked past Tolcheff into his bathroom and slammed the door. Tolcheff and the policeman were left staring at each other. 'It's all right, Mr Labrunie,' Tolcheff said, 'don't shoot me down. Just a professional dispute.'

When Draskovich came out, his face showing ugly red welts, Tolcheff was still standing by the door to the corridor. 'I'm sorry I did that,' he said.

'You're sorry.' Draskovich was whispering with such intensity that he spat in Tolcheff's face. 'You don't know how sorry you're going to be. Just don't ever come back to Russia, that's all I say. I'll give you to Petrov, I'll have you torn apart, so help me.'

He walked away and sat down at the table.

'We may not understand you,' Tolcheff said, his hand on the door, trying to speak calmly, 'but you sure don't understand us. I'm sorry I did that because it doesn't serve any purpose. I am sorry I didn't shoot you instead on the train. Now that I know how easy it is. You've shown me, you and your teapot.'

Draskovich pulled out his handkerchief and held it against

his face. 'Go away. Shoot me indeed. You had me in front of a pistol and you were pissing in your pants. I wasn't, you were. Pontebba. Just repeat that name to yourself, Pontebba.'

'Yes, I'm going,' Tolcheff said, opening the door. 'But listen carefully to this. You've broken the spell. So do forget the case Derkheim. If you lift a finger against her, or Anna, or me, I'll see to it that you get killed. By me or by one of my wormy friends. I swear it. You see, Draskovich, that was a starter pistol, in Pontebba. That's how lucky you are.'

He left.

LIII. Cannes, Rue d'Antibes

When Tolcheff came outside, the sky was black and a gusty, cold wind was blowing. He heard the rumble of thunder. How odd, in December.

He walked down the steps from the boulevard to the beach, and over the wet sand to the edge of the water. It was low tide. It did not make much difference, just a few feet of heavy, wet sand and pebbles laid bare.

He turned towards the sea with his hands in his pockets, he stared at the first lights going on in La Napoule and on the promontory, and he took such deep breaths that it hurt. Let the air blow right through me. He picked up a fistful of stones and threw them out as far as he could; the wind blew the sand and scraps of seaweed back into his face. He liked that, too, he would have liked to walk into the sea up to his hair and out again.

I'm a new man, I've won, done the right thing, we've saved Sophia and ourselves. It was luck, maybe, not astuteness. Nevertheless. Nonetheless. However. I've straightened myself out, that hodgepodge of ideas on violence and justice ... Precisely as I told him: he has broken a spell. Now he's afraid of me. Suddenly his body wasn't inviolable any more. Perhaps because of what he was going to say. Although I don't know what he was going to say. Perhaps because of the contempt he has for others, for everything, for life really, I guess.

Is that it? I'm not sure, but I'm not worried. I think I'll always know what to do now, without theorising.

He thought that Anna would tell from his face, the moment she laid eyes on him. There'll be no need for explanations. She will look at me, she will realise what happened to me, and choose to stick by me.

He found it hard to turn away. It was good standing there at the water line, the town invisible behind him, and this certainty in his grasp. Nuptiamus te, mare. If Draskovich offered me a choice of deaths, I'd take drowning. Maybe that proves I'm only part an inland man. Sea socialism.

He slowly walked towards the Gonnet hotel, following the dark beach. Above him were the brightly lit buildings; he was alone in another kind of night. Looking away, listening to the sea, he was on the shore of a desert island. Then he saw the name of the hotel high up and behind him, and he climbed back up to the boulevard, with a touch of fear or perhaps just of wanting to postpone the moment.

Anna was sitting by herself on the little hotel terrace, on a chair against the wall. The terrace was closed, all the other chairs had been taken inside. The white iron tables, bare, reflected the only light, which came from the lamps at each side of the entrance steps.

'I'm frozen,' she said when she saw him emerge from the shadowy front lawn. 'Let's leave, quickly.'

'Why are you out here?'

'I got tired of the lobby.' She pointed to the little suitcase standing at her feet. 'I checked out, for both of us. Let's go, let's get on our train to Marseilles now and go see Sophia. On the way, you can tell me everything that happened.'

'All right. But we're seeing the Judge first, remember?

He's in Super-Cannes, I found out where.'

He took her suitcase, and they started walking away from the sea, up the dark little street that ran alongside the hotel and ended at the Rue d'Antibes.

There was a silence. He hesitated to begin his account and she didn't press him.

It wasn't a bit the way I had foreseen it. She hardly looked at me. You make your little plans and you move yourself and all the players, as in a puppet theatre, but they live in their own worlds and put on their own plays. There's no connection between my thoughts and this girl, this separately alive person who has her own thirst and hunger and fear and desire. The tenderness I feel is for the girl I see, not for the girl SHE IS. And why should she want to follow me? What have I got to offer her? What do I have she needs?

Except a prick. He found satisfaction in hurting himself with that idea. It mostly comes too quick for her, and then, there are a few likes of it, some hundred million or so. How did Draskovich know, that night on the train . . . But he didn't let himself think that thought to the end.

They were in the Rue d'Antibes and blinked against the sudden brightness of its white gas lamps and Christmas shop-windows. It was the busiest hour of the day, with offices closing just then, people buying their little presents and all sorts of items for their Christmas dinners. The butchers and fishmongers had their wares out on the sidewalks on wooden tables and in baskets, with electric lights or blazing carbide lamps overhead. Pine branches and seaweed decorated cuts of meat, ducks, skinned rabbits, barrels of oysters and crabs. The customers were standing in line waiting, a crush spilling over from the sidewalks into the street, and everyone was talking, shaking hands, the merchants were making little jokes as they weighed the purchases and changed money. Next to a butcher or a bakery might be a luxurious shop with just one dress or a set of china in the window, with candles and red paper bells, and these places, too, were crowded with customers.

He turned to Anna because she stood still, and he looked

at her face in the warm light. She was observing a little girl in a bakery, who held a still smaller one by the hand, and who pointed out to the saleswoman a marzipan carrot in the window.

'Perhaps this is all this world has to offer,' Anna suddenly said, 'and perhaps it's enough.'

She walked on. 'I saw a woman before,' she added, 'who got herself just four oysters, and she was wearing a wedding ring, too. Two oysters each. She looked happy.'

'You mean, blessed are the poor, and how empty the hearts of the rich amidst their treasures?' His beach happiness had vanished. He felt quite heavy, a strange melancholy.

'Oh, screw,' Anna said. 'Anyway, it is Christmas to-morrow.'

They continued their way in silence. The shops were left behind, tall apartment houses lined the street. Then they crossed train tracks, on a narrow bridge, and found themselves amidst fields. The road continued paved, and another one turned off left, up the hill, with a blue and white metal road sign reading, Avenue de Vallauris. He took her arm for a moment to steer her that way, and they walked between villas in large dark gardens. 'They said it was half an hour, and no streetcar,' Tolcheff told her. 'Do you mind?'

She shook her head, he could just see the movement in the twilight that hung over the wide, silent avenue.

There was only rarely a street lamp now. The wind had died down, or perhaps they were in the lee of the hillside; not a branch stirred on the trees.

'What I meant was,' Anna said, 'she didn't need any world-wide vistas. And, the better your world would be, the more one's unhappiness would hurt.'

He did not answer, she didn't know if he had heard her words. They came to a long, low building, different from the villas, right on the road, though behind a tall, black iron gate. He struck a match to read the name plate. 'Yes, this is it. The Hildesheimer Clinic.'

LIV. Super-Cannes, the Judge

They were shown into a waiting room with large couches and vases with ferns everywhere, and bound copies of the magazine *L'Illustration*. 'It isn't a bit like a hospital,' Anna whispered, 'more like an expensive law office.'

'When you're really rich, they disguise it when you're sick. Or even when you're dead.'

First a nurse came to look at them, then a sombre lady in a grey housekeeper's dress. Did the Judge expect them? No, they had just arrived, but it was important. No, they weren't relatives, but it was important.

'What name should I give?'

'Tolcheff.'

'The Judge is probably asleep.'

'He won't mind being wakened by us.'

'Well,' the lady said, 'if you take the responsibility. But if you're not family, only one can go in. That is the absolute rule of the clinic.'

Tolcheff and Anna looked at one another and both began to smile. There was some kind of neat symmetry about this; that in a way, was how it had all started. Going to see Draskovich the snob. This time Tolcheff didn't wait for her to say she wanted to go. He gave her the papers he was carrying in his pocket. 'You do it, Ann.'

The Judge wasn't sleeping. He was sitting up in bed, reading a novel. He had two night tables, one covered with medicine bottles, a kidney-shaped basin with cotton wool, tubes, and little boxes; his hands travelled back and forth to the other, on which there were fruits and chocolates.

He stared at Anna over his glasses, as the housekeeper

announced, now professionally gay, 'A visitor for you, Judge. A late one, but the later, the prettier, they say. Miss Tolcheff.'

'Please sit down,' the Judge said, assuming from Anna's papers that she was bringing the letters he had dictated in the morning.

The housekeeper left.

Anna pulled her chair quite close. 'Judge,' she said, 'I have here a request to Emile Loubet himself, asking a full pardon for Sophia Derkheim.'

A visible shock travelled through the Judge's body. 'What?' he asked. 'A request from whom? Who is Emile Loubet?'

'But Judge – Emile Loubet is the President of the French Republic. And the request comes from you. It wouldn't have any weight, from someone else.'

'Who are you? Are you mad?'

'I'm a friend of Sophia. She has many friends. You sign here.'

History repeating itself. The smell of rainy clothes, the puddle on the carpet; he saw that scene with breath-taking sharpness. He could taste his cigar again, cigar smoke and the sharp aroma of wetness, the big feet of that girl, and then suddenly, he thought he had forgotten, you don't remember pain, that incredible pain in his stomach, a stabbing but worse than a knife, as if he were stabbed with a sharp stone, struck with inhuman strength –

He looked at Anna's feet instead of her face. She had finally thrown away those pumps that had belonged to Wenda and never did fit; she was wearing little sandals she had bought in the market. There was some consolation in that they were small and pretty.

'If you want to shoot, shoot,' he told her, and pressed the bell. He closed his eyes.

Anna had a soft laugh that made him open his eyes again. 'Sophia's had her chance,' she said. 'I just want your signature.'

At these words the Judge felt warm, a wave of warmth

from his feet to his head. I had turned stone cold, he thought; and that made him furious.

'Never, never!' he shouted. 'How dare you? Never. Nothing will give me more pleasure than seeing your friend rot and die in prison. Nothing will ever make me sign that.'

'But it is Christmas tomorrow.' Anna said.

The Judge closed his eyes once more. He wasn't going to say another word. He still had his finger on the bell.

'Judge,' she then said gently, as if waking him, 'won't even "Mon Repos" make you sign?'

He stared at her.

'That's where you mean to retire to, isn't it?'

The housekeeper burst in without knocking and looked from one to the other.

'The Judge would like some tea,' Anna informed her.

'Sir, if you don't mind taking your finger off the bell,' she replied icily. 'I'll see if there is still someone in the kitchen.' And she banged the door behind her.

'We know all about it,' Anna went on. 'And we know the editor who'd be dying to print the story.'

The Judge was silent. He closed his novel and studied the back cover. He took some kind of toffee out of his mouth and put it in the kidney-shaped basin. 'Who told you?' he finally asked.

'Draskovich,' Anna told him happily.

'Draskovich. Draskovich! The mischief-maker. Why?'

'Oh, he must have been dying to get at you. Not directly, of course. Through people like us.'

'But I've never put a straw in his way,' the Judge said, in a tone of voice as if still pleading for Draskovich to be more discreet.

Anna shrugged. 'How can you tell? You people have so many irons in so many fires . . . You must have crossed some scheme of his somewhere, at some time.'

'Was it difficult?' Tolcheff asked her as they walked down the Avenue de Vallauris again.

'No. What else could he do? But I think I was good. I enjoyed it. Aren't you pleased with me?'

He stopped to kiss her on her cheek. 'Now it's me who's sorry in a way. Remember when you said that it's hateful to play their sleazy games? When I was waiting there, in the middle of all those ferns, I thought I'd rather have kidnapped him, to make him sign.'

She took his hand and started walking faster down the street.

'It's the new me,' he said. 'The teapot me.'

'The what?' She waved the papers at him. 'But it's done, and I'm happy. It's all over. We can't out-torture them. But I think now I understand it all. When I was sitting at the Judge's bed. Don't you see that we're not playing their shabby games? They've spun their webs and there they sit, and they're such crooks, such *realists* as they'd call it; and the way to get them is through their own crookedness. No, but don't you see? You'd have wanted to go in and wave some more pistols at that Judge? But we've glued him in his own spider web. And right now he's trying to figure out how to get even with Draskovich, I bet you. There's your weapon! With my compliments.'

'Tell me, Ann, did he have one of those tubes in him, you know, when they feed you intravenously?'

'What? No.'

'It's what they do now. I saw it all in my mind, back there in that fern room. It seemed just the kind of thing for the Hildesheimer Clinic. And I'd pull the needle out of his arm, and stand beside him and have him sign the papers, or else watch him slowly die. Sorry, I'm talking nonsense. You're right.'

'No needle. He was eating toffees and reading Guy de Maupassant.'

'Oh. Let's run.'

LV. Cannes, the railroad station (II)

After they had crossed the railroad bridge and were back in the Rue d'Antibes, the rain started. It rained softly for a few minutes and they walked on. She gave him the petition to put in his inside pocket. But then it began to pour. A hard, cold rain lashed down into the street, and they ducked under the awning of a shop.

Anna saw they were standing in front of the same baker where she had seen the girls buy their marzipan carrot. All was dark now, and the street lay empty in front of them, lit only by the gas lamps at the corners. Even the apartments on the upper floors seemed dark and empty, until she noticed the edges of light where curtains weren't closed all the way. I wished we had watched longer, or bought something ourselves, to remember this street as it was then.

A man in a black oilskin coat rode by on a bicycle, splashing water to each side. The road was already flooded in places.

'Quarter to nine,' Tolcheff said. 'We have to move on, if want to see Zidkin.' He clasped her suitcase under one arm, took her hand, and they ran down the deserted street, as close as possible to the houses.

At the corner of the station square, the rain abruptly turned to hail, large stones which hammered down on the shiny pavement and jumped in all directions. 'Wait,' she asked, 'we've got five minutes. I've lost my breath.'

They stood in a doorway and looked out over the large square where nothing stirred. One electric lamp, hanging from a cross wire, silhouetted the streaks of hail and showed up the emptiness of that black space. 'Good-bye Cannes,' she said. He put his collar up and announced, 'I'm going to be[?] or steal or buy a coat in Marseilles tomorrow, or I'll die of pneumonia.' 'My rabbit's already drowned,' she told him.

It was approaching nine. They raced across and bough[t] two tickets for the Marseilles train.

The next one was due to leave at ten. Anna was to g[o] ahead to the westbound platform and get into the firs[t] third-class carriage; Zidkin, about to arrive, obviousl[y] shouldn't see her. If Tolcheff didn't show up in time, sh[e] would get off again.

But he boarded the train, which was formed at half pas[t] nine, only a minute after her. He shivered and dried himsel[f] as well as he could with his handkerchief.

He waved it at her. 'Draskovich's red and yellow.'

'I've got us two sandwiches,' Anna said.

He looked around. 'What a lousy train!'

'We've come down in the world, Andrew. From the to[p] to the bottom. Never mind, it's a train.'

They were in a third class of the old type, divided int[o] narrow compartments by waist-high partitions, with benche[s] of wood, and the entire carriage lit by two Argand oil lamps[,] one at each end. The only other passengers were arm[y] recruits, farmers' sons in ill-fitting new uniforms, snoring i[n] their corners. It was Christmas Eve.

'I told Zidkin I had booked him in my room at th[e] Gonnet,' Tolcheff reported, 'and that he shouldn't be in an[y] hurry to go and see Drasky. I said Drasky was in a viciou[s] mood and had sent me back to my post right away, an[d] would surely do the same to him, the moment he laid eye[s] on him.'

'You haven't told me yet what really happened wit[h] Draskovich,' Anna said.

'No . . . I will. Anyway, Zidkin asked, "Then why didn'[t] you wire me to call off the press conference? And here I wa[s] so pleased I wasn't stopped." I said there had been no poin[t,] Draskovich already knew Zidkin had sent in a report on him[.] "How is that possible?" he asked. He looked a bit scare[d] then, but not as much as I'd have thought. I answered that

170

didn't know, some enemy of his at the embassy perhaps. Draskovich had talked of Zidkin floating down the Seine, no less. "Don't worry," I said, "he isn't doing so well. I saw the Judge, and I hear Draskovich is rather discredited." You see, I'm learning your recipe, and it works. Specially because Zidkin has changed. He was with that girl he has found here, Françoise, and she is nice. Not at all what you'd expect. You can tell he's worried and maybe ashamed about his job now, with her around. I had thought she'd be some kind of chippy, leading him on, but not at all. Imagine, Zidkin . . .'

'You see. There's hope for everybody.'

'Yes,' he said, almost wistfully. 'He asked after you, "What a shame Draskovich got himself such a good-looking girl," he said. And he's only seen you asleep, with your mouth open.'

'But what about the press conference?'

'Yes, I mustn't leave that out. Three journalists came.'

He laughed at the face she made. 'It didn't matter. Everything is fine. You see, one of them was from Havas, the news agency, and one from the Figaro. So it'll be in all the newspapers all right. The third man was from a little local paper, the Eclair-Pyrénées. Zidkin has it all noted down in a report, they'll love reading that. He never delivered the speech he had prepared, for the Havas and the Figaro man just picked up the text and said thank you and left. And then he and the Eclair-Pyrénées man were sitting face to face in an empty office, with a couple of waiters carrying in the pâté and lobster salad and white wine for twenty that he had ordered.'

'He didn't bring some of it with him by chance?'

'I suggested he wait a while before presenting the bill.'

'Well, we did it, we did it,' Anna said. 'She's safe.'

The train got into motion, very slowly and painfully. The soldier across from them in the corner shifted and moaned in his sleep. The Argand lamps started swinging in small circles, throwing elongated shadows across the yellow wooden slats of the roof.

LVI. Marseilles, Hôtel de la Gare

Their train arrived in Marseilles at daybreak. It was still raining.

'We got here,' she said. 'I can't believe it. Did you notice, there was one farmhouse, with at least five cows, and the train didn't stop?'

'An oversight.'

They put their arms around each other as they came out of the station. Church bells were ringing through the wet air, the empty street reverberated with their sound.

'Merry Christmas,' she said.

'It's too early to go see Sophia.'

'It's too early for anything. Do we have money for a hotel room?'

'But Ann. Of course.'

They entered a side street. A sign beside the entrance to a high, sombre building read, 'Grand Hôtel de la Gare. Tous Conforts.' She looked up along its façade, licking the rain from her lips.

'Is it all right to take one room?' he asked her.

'Oh, please. I'm freezing. I'd be dizzy up there alone.'

Did they want running water, the clerk asked.

Were there bathrooms?

'But certainly. On each floor. And a water closet.'

'We don't need running water then,' Tolcheff said.

'Room 607. One franc ten per night.'

They were taken up in the open grille elevator, and then were alone in a little room, with a bed, a chair, and a table with a washbasin and an oil lamp on it. Along the wall ran a pipe which was hot to the touch. The window had shutters which were nearly closed; over the bed hung a picture of a slender young woman in a long skirt shaking an apple tree, while a little girl was watching. 'Souvenir de Mortefontaine,' it said under it.

He pushed the shutters out and looked over the tangle of wet roofs of the old town around them. A million rooms, a million people. A million fates. He felt uneasy, lost, half sick. 'Come look,' he said to Anna, who was standing beside the bed, her eyes on the picture of the woman and the child.

She came to the window. 'The bed's clammy and dirty.'

'Not dirty. Just greyish. Let's dry our clothes on that pipe.'

They hung up everything and jumped in bed. 'Hold me tight,' she said.

He crept on top of her and then let himself roll sideways. They stayed like that, looking at each other, he in her, without moving.

'Let's stay like this for an hour,' he whispered.

'You know, I've got used to your body, all those bones sticking out. It's exciting.'

'Anita. That was the name of Garibaldi's wife.'

'Is that how you see us?'

'It's the same name, Anna, Anita.'

She put her hands behind him and rolled back. 'Make love to me,' she said. 'Do it, do it.'

She came, and looking hard at him, reached him with one hand and stroked him until he did, too. 'Good,' she said.

They lay still, and he now heard that the church bells were still ringing. 'Did our journey change you, Anita?' he suddenly asked.

'Yes.'

'How?'

'Trains, machines . . . Don't you agree that in a building with electric light you couldn't have ghosts? I was secure in our express, flying along at sixty miles an hour. More secure than in my old bed in Petersburg.'

It serves me right. Ann would give a clear answer to a sloppy question. But I had hoped she would have said something about not being lonely any more. Something

173

about me, not about machines.

'Don't you agree?' she now insisted.

'Well, no. I don't think electric light chases any ghosts away. Not the real ones. When I die, I'd rather be in a room with a candle than under an electric light. I thought that was what you meant, too – when you were comparing Dvinsk and Cannes. I think only people can take away our fears.'

She shook her head without lifting it from the pillow. 'Oh, I didn't mean any of that stuff. Don't get all wistful, Andrew. I'm just happy with speed, and with steel and glass around me.'

'But I'm not wistful. Machines diminish us. Maybe they do make it easier not to think of ghosts and of death, but that makes death the more frightening when it comes. Before there were machines, people moved differently, with more confidence.'

She gave a dissatisfied sigh.

'Since they put streetcars on Nevski Prospect,' he said, 'you can't walk there. To give an example.'

'What? But you're not that fat.'

'Be serious now. Don't you understand what I mean? You can go along there, move, march, but not walk. What can racing along at sixty miles an hour do for you? Just look up at a blue sky instead, it circles the whole earth in one day.'

She sat up and stared at the sky outside their window as if to test his words. 'But there's no such thing! There's nothing! It's just an optical illusion, because blue rays refract more, or less, I forgot which. God, you're a sentimentalist, this has been very bad for you.'

'And you're a schoolteacher all right. "Blue rays refract more." '

She laughed. 'Yes, I am a schoolteacher.'

He kissed the line where the curve of her breast began, and let himself fall back. 'The softness of a woman,' he said in a low voice. 'The only reason I like trains, too, I think the only reason men build these enormous engines, is as a counter, a counterpoint, to the softness of women.'

She looked down on him with big, round eyes.

'You can laugh,' he said. 'But I do love you. You're my train madonna.'

'Like a saint for sailors? I'd like that.'

LVII. Marseilles, the prison

'Visits are allowed only on the first Monday of each month,' they were told. Anyway, most of the women prisoners were in the common room for a Christmas solemnity.

But as they had come for legal as well as personal reasons, and they were friends of Sophia Derkheim all the way from Russia – of course, they could come back, but since it was Christmas, and they had good news . . .

They were told to wait.

'It's nice and warm here,' Anna said. Their clothes, which had come off the radiator pipe stiff and warm, were soaked again. It had been a long walk from the last streetcar stop to Sophia's prison, in the unending fine rain. They were sitting in a guardroom, near a potbellied stove attended by the only man on duty, who, with his jacket unbuttoned, picked his teeth and regularly muttered, 'Guard duty on Christmas – '

'I think you should go in alone,' Tolcheff said. 'She hardly knows me.'

But Anna refused that.

An orderly appeared and told them to follow him. 'Leave that newspaper here.' That was *Le Petit Marseillais*, a paper that had appeared on the streets at noon. On an inside page it carried the Zidkin-Grunwald statement about Sophia, French justice, and Christmas spirit forgiveness, almost complete.

They were led to a bare room with four kitchen chairs. Its only window had been painted over with thick, flaking, white paint, and most of its light came from an electric bulb hanging from the ceiling. On one wall was a clock, and a placard listed a long series of regulations.

A door opened and in came Sophia, followed by a prison matron, who sat down in a corner.

'Anna!' Sophia cried.

They fell into each other's arms.

'Let me look at you,' Anna finally said, taking a step backward. 'Oh, I'm glad. You look well.'

'Yes, I'm all right,' Sophia said, wiping her eyes.

'And this is Andrew Tolcheff, remember?'

They kissed, too.

'They don't treat you too rotten?' Tolcheff asked.

'No, not really. We sew all day.' She held up her hands, which were full of red needle pricks. 'Of course not today. We were about to light the candles.'

In an odd way, Sophia did look well. The prison food and the lack of sun and air had made her face even thinner and had given her skin a shiny pallor; with her burning eyes, it gave her a kind of beauty, as of a saint in an El Greco painting. Anna thought that perhaps the prison regime, the impossibility of free will, had forced a certain peacefulness on Sophia for the first time in her life.

They sat down and Anna related the story of the extradition plan and how it had been sidetracked. Sophia stared at them as if she couldn't believe what she was told. She was becoming more and more nervous. 'But we tell you, the danger is past, for sure,' Anna said. 'It's in the paper today.'

'Can I see it?'

'We weren't allowed to bring it in. We'll try again on the way out, to leave it for you.'

'You can be sure,' Tolcheff said, taking her hand.

A silence. Sophia grumbled something about why didn't they leave her alone. Then she reddened and said, 'And you two travelled all this way, just to help me!'

Anna laughed, a gay laugh that made the matron look up with surprise. 'You don't have to worry about that, dear Sophia. It wasn't a sacrifice, it was a good journey. And I had to do it for myself as much as for you. That man, the Undersecretary, had, had humiliated me.'

'How?' Sophia asked apprehensively.

'Oh, that's hard to explain. Nothing physical. Worse, I think.' And turning to Tolcheff, she asked, 'We didn't really get even with him, did we?'

'It'll need a revolution for that.'

'And you?' Sophia asked him.

'I – I owe your brother more than a train journey. We'll do more, too, I promise you. I'm going on to Brussels from here. Things will be different.'

Then even Anna and Sophia seemed to find nothing further to say to each other. The matron cleared her throat, as if about to call an end to the visit, when Anna yelled, 'Wait! There's more. You tell her, Andrew.'

'The Judge,' Tolcheff began, 'your Judge, so to speak – '

'Yes?'

'He signed a petition yesterday, to the President of France, asking a pardon for you. It should have a very good chance, coming from him.'

Sophia was dumbfounded. 'What? Can I read it?'

'We didn't bring it. I was afraid someone might confiscate it here. You must tell us who your lawyer was, and then we will take it to him.'

'Oh . . .'

'But you don't seem pleased,' Anna said, bewildered.

'Well, yes, of course. It just seems so strange that he'd do that. As if he weren't taking me seriously, as if it had been a children's game. I can assure you, if he hadn't been such a pathetic old man, I would have killed him. I'm a very good shot.'

'We forced him, we forced him!' Anna cried. 'It isn't a bit like that. He's an old crook, we got a hold on him because of a scandal we heard about.'

Sophia still had a vague look about her. Did she think these sordid goings on spoiled the purity of her case?

'Believe me, he hates you,' Anna added.

'You know,' Sophia finally answered, 'I don't think I

really minded the idea of being here for the full term of my sentence. It's a grim place, don't think it isn't. But I'm a political, as they call it, and they treat me with some respect. I'm on my way to being someone. I know that sounds crazy. Please don't think I am ungrateful. You're the best friend I ever had. The only one.'

She embraced Anna again.

'But you know, I understand very well,' Anna said, addressing Tolcheff over Sophia's shoulder. 'It is security, you're covered in the back. Your jail is like my train.'

Sophia was following her own thoughts. 'If I come out now, they'll say, what a fuss about so little. I wanted the weight of that year, not for myself, but for my future work . . .' Her voice trailed off.

'Well, but damn it,' Tolcheff said, 'we'll just tear up the damn thing. Let's be Machiavellian. If it's better for you, better for your reputation, if you want to be an activist, do the year.'

Sophia sat down again, blew her nose, and then shook her head. 'No,' she said softly. 'That's nonsense, don't you think? I wouldn't work that way if I didn't have to. If I can get out, I couldn't stick it one more day. It's no hotel, believe me.'

'Also, suppose that – ' Tolcheff was going to say that if Draskovich was after all not as defeated as they thought, she wouldn't be safe in the prison. But he swallowed the rest of his sentence.

'My defence lawyer's name was Maître Thibault. He was very nice. He lives in Cannes, his office is on the Rue d'Antibes.'

'Well, we know where that is,' Anna said, taking Sophia's hand. 'You do want us to take the petition to him, then?'

'It's really the best thing to do,' Tolcheff added.

Sophia nodded vehemently.

LVIII. Marseilles, and the marshes of Ravenna

It had stopped raining when they walked back to the streetcar stop. The rain clouds were being blown out to sea against a sky of a high, even whiteness. The puddles in the street gleamed, and the patches of grass were greener in the sharp light.

'Well . . . ,' Anna said.

'You didn't want her to be all overcome with gratitude, did you?' Tolcheff asked. 'That would have been terrible. We're no liberal do-gooders, we're a kind of soldier in a kind of war.'

'You, maybe. I'm not. Don't think I don't still like her.'

'Neither gratitude nor revenge. Bakunin.'

'You admit we didn't revenge ourselves on Draskovich?'

'As we said before. Yes, I admit. That needs a revolution.'

'And that's why you're going to Brussels.'

He scrutinised her face. 'Are you being ironic? Anyway, the answer is yes. Although cause and effect may be far removed in time and in place.'

She put her hand on his arm. 'I didn't mean to be ironic. When are you going?'

'As soon as they've answered my cable, and wired me my train money. Anita? You're coming with me after all, aren't you?'

She shook her head. 'I must go back home, to my school.'

'Perhaps you think I'm getting carried away with myself, with this Anita business. . . . I'm not. I know you're Ann. It's just nice to call you Anita. She was an amazing woman. She was right with him in all the battles. With Garibaldi, I mean. She had a baby in the middle of a guerrilla war. And she died in the marshes of Ravenna, while they were being chased by half the Austrian army.'

Anna's soft laugh. Shy perhaps, insulating herself.

'I don't make it sound very attractive, I guess,' he said.

'Andrew, don't worry about comparing yourself to Garibaldi. You'll do as much as he did if you get the chance. It's me. I'm not a guerrilla fighter, I'm a schoolteacher.'

'Ann Anita, all that was ages ago. Things are different now. I want to take you to Brussels, not to the marshes of Ravenna.'

'I'm not being literal, Andrew. Won't your life unroll itself, and end, in the marshes of Ravenna?'

'The moment he saw – ' Tolcheff began before he had even understood her words. Then he listened to them within himself, and was silent.

He watched his feet, the life of their own they led, passing one another over the cobblestones, which were still slippery.

She looked away, too. I wish I had not said that.

'The moment he saw her,' Tolcheff finished, 'he said, "tu devi esser mia." You ought to be mine. It should be that simple.'

She sighed. 'Sometimes I think this is going to be the wrong century for you altogether.'

'It happened in a town on the coast of Brazil. He had rowed ashore from his warship. She was an eighteen-year-old virgin.'

'That's history? Virginity and all?'

He laughed. 'Absolutely. Attested to after years of research by a team of German professors. You know how they really get into things.'

'Well, Andrew, you're sure more like Garibaldi than I like an eighteen-year-old virgin.'

He stopped smiling again. He looked pale suddenly, dark eyes in a pinched face. 'I used to be alone, but I never minded, I preferred it, I think. But it's different now. Getting on a train to Brussels without you gives me the shivers. On the beach in Cannes, yesterday, I was so sure. About you, I mean.'

She took his hand and did not answer.

'There's the streetcar,' she said. 'Let's run for it.'

When they were back in their room on the sixth floor of the Hôtel de la Gare, the sun was out. Everywhere gutters and pipes were gurgling and dripping; attic windows were opened and laundry appeared on balconies. The zinc of the flat roofs reflected the blue sky, even the slating shone.

'Look, they've brought us two towels.' Anna said.

'They're giving us very nice smiles downstairs. They must think we're newlyweds. Or maybe a couple on a secret assignation in the big city.'

'From some muddy little town where my husband is the notary.'

'But he's bound to get an anonymous letter.'

'And then he'll turn me out into the street and steal my dowry.'

'And one day I'll find you shivering in a doorway, a common harlot.'

She was pacing through the room, biting her nails which he had never seen her do, and standing still every time she passed the picture of the woman, the child, and the apple tree. 'I wish I could steal it and take it with me.' she said, staring at it. 'It's so sweet, and longing . . . Like life when you're very young.'

'Well, let's.'

'No. I want other people to lie in this bed and see it.'

He came over to her. 'Lift your arms, he asked, and gently took off her dress.

He made love to her without thinking about himself, overwhelmed with love for her sadness. It's unbearable to see her at a loss. That was my discovery, the night of the Venetian Alps in the moonlight. I must not ever try to get the better of her.

'Are you cold?' he asked.

'No, I like being naked.'

'Wasn't it nice?'

'It was lovely,' she said.

'Don't you think the way people make love proves something? I mean, in the beginning I behaved like a schoolboy, but now I could – I mean, it's not a physical thing. Wouldn't it be stupid then to separate, just at this point?'

She lifted herself on her elbow and looked down on him as she had done after they had made love that morning. 'But you'll be back,' she said. 'Just ring my bell, and I'll open the door, I promise, and let you make love to me. Day or night.'

'And if there's someone else there?'

'We'll throw him out. Come on, Andrew. Smile.'

She was still talking through the echo of those fatal words she should not have spoken, on their way to the streetcar stop. To die in the marshes of Ravenna.

He did smile. I must not talk to her of loneliness again. It's a poor argument, and a cruel one.

LIX. Marseilles, the harbour

Wandering through narrow streets, they had suddenly seen masts of ships sticking out, in a gap between two tall buildings. Steering for those had led them to the harbour basin.

Here the horizon was blocked by the towers of two huge fortresses which straddled the entrance to the harbour. The waterway was curved, and that made it seem as if these were right next to each other; a strip of sky in between them was purple from the setting sun. Only when you craned your neck could you see a ribbon of grey, the sea – or maybe only the evening fog over it. It was Anna who had kept them walking, for she now felt she had to know where she was and collect images from this other world.

They had seen the new part of town first, going in the opposite direction of the prison.

There, wide, tree-lined streets lay very quiet in this late afternoon of Christmas Day.

Sometimes the curtains weren't drawn in a downstairs room and they saw people eating around a table, or children playing. Once they heard piano music as a door opened to let in a man and a woman. A cab slowly drove past, the coachman looking hopefully at them.

A leaden silence, a silence of childhood fears.

At the harbour it was different. No sign of Christmas: on and around the ships men were working, and there was a heavy traffic of carts and wagons. The little bars everywhere were crowded, with their doors open to the street. A sharp wind blew from the water, the sky was clear with a first star high over their heads, and the blinding flash of the lighthouse sweeping through it at every count of three.

The pavements slippery with all sorts of indefinable debris, a smell of dampness and rotting and urine.

She wanted to go into a bar and drink a glass of wine, but she turned back in the doorway when she saw there were only men inside. A boy came up to them and whispered something to Tolcheff, who shook his head and said, 'Get lost.'

'What did he want?'

'Nothing.'

'No, tell me, couldn't we have given him something?'

'He offered to take us to a place where you can see a woman make love with a donkey. "Fifty centimes a person," he said.'

'Oh – '

'Well, you wanted to know.'

'How disgusting. It's a filthy town.'

'They're just poor devils. Look at those houses they have to live in. That's more disgusting.'

'Let's go to church,' she said. 'It *is* Christmas.'

They turned inland again and presently came to a little

183

church they had passed before, an old building sitting on a knoll, with granite steps leading up to it. There was light behind its windows, but when they had climbed up to it, they found the doors locked.

'Well then, let's go see the lady and the donkey instead,' Tolcheff suggested.

'Are you serious?'

'No.'

LX. Cannes, Tolcheff

Back in Cannes, this time they stayed in a boarding house on the Rue Saint-Dizier, where the fishermen live. A passenger on the train from Marseilles had given them the address.

They went to see Sophia's lawyer and handed him the petition. When they were out in the street again, Tolcheff said, 'Now I have a present for you,' and gave her a Cannes–Saint Petersburg ticket for the winter express.

She reddened. 'No, I don't want that,' she told him, 'it's disgusting. I'm going back third class.'

'Ann. That's the second time I've ever seen you blush. I want you to go back the same way – since you want to go back. Please. Once more, and without Draskovich, and without me to pester you. To finish – well, whatever it is you're after.'

'But how did you get it?'

'I managed. I've enough left to wait for the train fare from Brussels. And you must take this.' And he gave her five ten-franc pieces.

She looked at them in her hand. 'No.'

'Don't fuss. I promised you, remember. The dining car. Another thing, don't worry about Draskovich. He's not going to bring this up again in his department.'

'No, I won't worry.' She went on slowly shaking her head, staring at the money.

'You'll see me back, you know,' Tolcheff said. 'I'll get myself a passport in Brussels.'

'Of course I'll see you back. Please be careful.'

'And the offer stands?'

It took her a second to understand. 'Oh yes. It stands. All hours. Pull the bell three times, that's for me.'

Her train left Cannes at four in the afternoon. It was as sunny and mild a day as their first one there, but they were too nervous and restless to go anywhere. They wouldn't admit it to themselves, but they were relieved when it was time to go to the station.

He put her suitcase in the compartment for her. She had a lower berth this time, and the upper berth wasn't made up but locked against the wall. 'The train is almost empty, miss, you will have all the space you need,' the attendant said.

Tolcheff had bought her a little paperback novel, which he pulled out of his pocket and put in her seat with a self-conscious smile. It is not a role that suits me.

It was half past three.

'Please go now,' she said, 'it's too nerve-racking.'

'Bye, Anita.' He kissed her lightly and got off.

He left the platform without looking back, and walked out of the station and down to the Esplanade once more.

I'll be off too, soon. Tomorrow the money should come. Then Brussels. I'll speak my mind with them. I'll defend a different policy for the future. Less wormy.

But there was something lifeless about his thoughts. He didn't continue them. He just walked down that sloping street, all you have to do is roll your legs like those children's toys they pull after them. He came to the Croisette, and started to cross it, looking at the sea. The sun, already low, threw long shadows at him.

He heard a shout, and was pulled sharply by the arm; a carriage went by so close that its door handle scraped him and tore off the middle button of Draskovich's tweed jacket.

The cabman turned around and shouted, 'Watch it, you idiot, you'll get yourself killed.'

'That was a near thing,' the man who had grabbed his arm said.

'Thank you. I thank you very much.'

Two young women were travelling in the cab, and they were still looking back at him with furious faces. I frightened them. They're pretty. One of those carriages Draskovich talked about so. His sensuous promenade, the thrills of life I'll never know.

I'm not doing very well on it, I must admit. The first time, dragging Ann along half asleep. The second time, nearly run over.

He sat down on one of the little chairs the municipality places along the sea boulevard, facing the Mediterranean.

He closed his eyes, tilted his face towards the sun, and sat motionless. He didn't hear a sound behind him, as if the Croisette were empty now. The last carriage, and it missed me.

Now rearrange my thoughts. I'm simply back to what I was. I used to be all right. This can't throw me, or my ideas were all phoney.

A girl's narrow middle.

But I never wanted private little happinesses. I want to work for a change in the bloody mess this world is in. And it is not the other way around. It isn't that I want to, because I can't find peace within my own life. If that were my motive, then there's no hope, then all of us are doomed to live out our days in, in shells of selfishness.

I'm not afraid to look back into my own life, I'm not escaping into justice like my sister escapes in diplomatic receptions.

No, damn it. Let's look the worst in the eye then, let the worst be true. Let my father be a slob who knocked up my mother or let my mother be a floozy who didn't know for sure who my father was. Let them both not have cared a damn about me.

And so what.

Those two seeds got together by fate and from that moment on, the sum total was me, and to hell with them, that is when I began. They gave me life and the rest is up to me. I don't want any advantages quote unquote. I don't want anything more than a child begging along the roads of Bengal.

Garibaldi was no revolutionary, let me admit it. He was a patriot, a nice one because he had no country yet. Just a brave liberal.

These are new times.

The world is watching me. I have to show now that it's not all a fraud. There is a mysterious inner logic to things, and perhaps I am the test case. The case of Tolcheff versus Draskovich, balancing the world.

And God help us, or better, God can't help us, if we don't deliver. We must –

He felt a tap on his arm.

An old woman in black, with a book of what looked like theatre tickets. Then it could also have been Ann come back, I got off the train, I had to.

Please, Ann, please have done that. Be on your way down that street. You could already have been this woman here. Give me that, and then I don't mind anything, then I don't mind Ravenna.

'The chair, sir. It's fifteen centimes.'

'Oh – is it? I didn't know.' He made a show of searching through his pockets, though he knew he didn't have a penny left. The woman watched him patiently.

'I'm afraid I have nothing on me,' he said.

'I'm sorry, sir. But – '

'That's all right.'

And he got up and started to walk slowly along the boulevard, towards where the sun was already touching the clouds that always seemed to pile up over the western horizon at this hour, on these warm winter days.

LXI. Between Cannes and Genoa, Anna

When the day ended, the Petersburg Express was still following the shoreline. They had passed the border, and were in Italy. The Riviera di Ponente, the coast of the setting sun, Tolcheff had told her it was called. But the sun was setting behind them and the sea was dark. The wine-coloured sea. Now, running east, the train corridor was on the side of the water and she had been standing there for hours, half leaning against the glass. She was very tired and glad when it got dark, when she could go and sit down in her compartment; for some reason she had decided she had to stand there and look at the sea as long as possible.

It had been disappointing that it hadn't been the same as before, that her compartment window faced inland.

She tucked her feet under her in her favourite position. She looked at the lights blinking, the houses close to the tracks, most of them dark with one lit window, the kitchen; then dark fields, and on a hilltop a farm with a stone archway and a lamp in it. She had the feeling she had seen that same house on the way out, going west, that they had both seen it at the same moment. Across the corridor – the Italian train from Genoa had had no curtain. He had said – she forgot. But only now, through the lamp shining against that curve of large grey stones, did her thoughts return to Tolcheff. Till then, she had not let him enter her mind.

But, she thought, I'm not miserable, I approach the idea of being miserable, I almost touch it, like a child with an object she's forbidden to play with. I could very easily throw myself at it. It would be a nice relief. But I won't.

My train will help. It's a good thing it is a different train.

Not just turned around. This rug, for instance, is different. There's another cupboard. A picture of the Eiffel Tower. One of the Mona Lisa. I'm in no one's power, only in that of an engine sweeping me along, gliding me along, with thousands of horsepower. I must find out how much. I would like to know the precise number. A round steel machine.

It was dark outside, the window only showed her reflection. She opened the book Tolcheff had bought her; it was titled *Pauline*, by George Sand.

'There are people who are only happy when they are dreaming; they lack that store of patience that makes the imperfection of human beings acceptable.'

When she got up to go to the restaurant car, she took her book along but decided to leave her ratty coat.

The corridors were silent this time. An old man and a child holding his hand were looking out at the darkness reflecting the corridor lights. They pressed themselves against the glass to let her pass, without turning their heads around at her.

The tables were laid with white linen. The vases, some with little roses, others with the three carnations she remembered.

The head waiter led her to a table for two.

On the table behind her stood a little silver vase with carnations. Her table had roses. She stood up and switched the vases.

The only other passenger was a man eating in the far corner. When she caught his eye, he tried a little smile on her. She frowned and moved to the other chair at her table, with her back towards him. She felt embarrassed for him as she did that, but then thought, well, damn him, he makes me ride backwards. This table is on the other side of the train, though. I'm on the sea side again.

She cupped her face against the windowpane, but when she finally distinguished something in the darkness, it was a shadowy cluster of buildings with lamps here and there. We've turned inland.

'Where are we?' she asked the waiter who came with the menu.

'Nearing Genoa, madam.'

She ordered dinner. 'Do you have Nuits Saint Georges?' she asked.

'Yes, we do, madam. A half bottle?'

'A whole one, please.'

He brought her the wine, poured a glass, and waited for her approval. She drank, and nodded hastily.

Then, after he had left, she leaned her face against the window, and she started to cry.

But when the waiter came back with the first course, she was quietly reading her book.

Peterborough, New Hampshire, 7 August 1974

Also on the Adventure/Thriller list

RED LIGHT RED

As told to ALAN RADNOR

SOME STORIES OF SUBVERSION AND COR-
RUPTION IN HIGH PLACES ARE SO EXPLOSIVE
THAT NO NEWSPAPER OR MAGAZINE, NO
TELEVISION OR RADIO PROGRAMME CAN
HANDLE THEM. THEY CAN ONLY BE PUBLISHED
IN THE FORM OF FICTION. *RED LIGHT RED* IS
SUCH A STORY . . .

Call her 'Sandra Brown'. Or 'Rochelle Duvalle'. Neither
is her real name but she used both. Attractive, intelligent,
idealistic, already an experienced prostitute by the time
she came to the attention of Soviet 'sexpionage' experts,
she was perfect to front the most audacious wide-scale
mission of subversion ever mounted against a Western
power. The total destruction of the authority of the
British 'Establishment' by the setting-up and exposure of
many of its most important members as sexual deviates.

Presented as a gripping, authentic thriller, RED LIGHT
RED is firmly based on inside knowledge of the 'dirty
tricks' of the major intelligence agencies – and of a major
Soviet plot of recent years to subvert the British
'Establishment' that came terrifyingly close to success . . .

0 7221 7197 8   £1.10

ADVENTURE/THRILLER

A selection of bestsellers from SPHERE

Fiction

SHARKEY'S MACHINE	William Diehl	£1.50	☐
WAR STORY	Gordon McGill	£1.00	☐
THE GLENDOWER LEGACY	Thomas Gifford	£1.25	☐
BAAL	Robert McCammon	95p	☐
SEASON OF PASSION	Danielle Steel	£1.25	☐

Film and TV tie-ins

SATURN 3	Steve Gallagher	95p	☐
THE PROFESSIONALS 5: BLIND RUN	Ken Blake	85p	☐
THE PROFESSIONALS 6: FALL GIRL	Ken Blake	85p	☐
THE PROFESSIONALS 7: HIDING TO NOTHING	Ken Blake	85p	☐
THE PROFESSIONALS 8: DEAD RECKONING	Ken Blake	85p	☐
THE PROMISE	Danielle Steel	95p	☐

Non-Fiction

THE DAY THE BOMB FELL	Clyde W. Burleson	£1.25	☐
SECRETS OF OUR SPACESHIP MOON	Don Wilson	£1.10	☐
ARISTOTLE ONASSIS	Nicholas Fraser, Philip Jacobson, Mark Ottaway & Lewis Chester	£1.60	☐
SECRETS OF LOST ATLAND	Robert Scrutton	£1.50	☐

All Sphere books are available at your local bookshop or newsagent, or can be ordered direct from the publisher. Just tick the titles you want and fill in the form below.

Name...

Address ....

....

Write to Sphere Books, Cash Sales Department, P.O. Box 11, Falmouth, Cornwall TR10 9EN.

Please enclose cheque or postal order to the value of the cover price plus:

UK: 25p for the first book plus 12p per copy for each additional book ordered to a maximum charge of £1.05.

OVERSEAS: 40p for the first book and 12p for each additional book.

BFPO & EIRE: 25p for the first book plus 10p per copy for the next 8 books, thereafter 5p per book.

Sphere Books reserve the right to show new retail prices on covers which may differ from those previously advertised in the text or elsewhere, and to increase postal rates in accordance with the GPO.